IF WE'RE REALLY QUIET, IT WON'T FIND US

JOE HARVEY

MILFORD HOUSE

an imprint of Sunbury Press, Inc.
Mechanicsburg, PA USA

MILFORD HOUSE

an imprint of Sunbury Press, Inc.
Mechanicsburg, PA USA

For information about special discounts for bulk purchases, please contact Sunbury Press Orders Dept. at (855) 338-8359 or orders@sunburypress.com.

To request one of our authors for speaking engagements or book signings, please contact Sunbury Press Publicity Dept. at publicity@sunburypress.com.

ISBN: 978-1-62006-323-1 (Trade Paperback)

Library of Congress Control Number: 2019953713

FIRST MILFORD HOUSE PRESS EDITION: January 2020

Product of the United States of America
0 1 1 2 3 5 8 13 21 34 55

Set in Adobe Garamond
Designed by Crystal Devine
Cover by Riaan Wilmans
Edited by Lawrence Knorr

Continue the Enlightenment!

To the three amigos:
George, John, and Peter

Famous Last Words (idiom)
an ironic comment
to a seemingly sure situation
that may be proven wrong by events
(sometimes fatally)

I.

"COMPASS?"

"Check."

"Flashlight?"

"Check."

"Batteries?"

"Batteries . . . batteries," George said, looking over his camping supplies spread out in tidy rows on a tarp in the driveway. "Nope, no batteries. I must have used them on the last trip. I'll have my mom pick some up at the store. Write that down on the shopping list, please."

"Okay." Abby put down the clipboard and picked up the spiral-bound notepad. "Batteries. What size?"

George checked the batteries in the flashlight. "'D.' What's next?"

She looked over the checklist. "Duct Tape. Why do you need duct tape?"

"You can use it for anything: to fix a hole in your shoe, mend a rip in your tent—I even used it to make a visor once when I forgot my hat."

"Really?"

"Yeah."

"Wow. Okay. Duct Tape."

"Check."

Abby lowered the clipboard. "Why don't you just have your mom or dad pack your stuff for you? My mom's packing my stuff for me right now."

"My dad wants me to be prepared. He says that the only way you're going to survive in an emergency is if you have the right gear and you know how to use it. And that starts with knowing what's in your backpack. If someone else packs it for you, you won't know what's in it, let alone how to use it—no offense. I really appreciate your help."

"None taken, I'm happy having my mom pack my stuff for me. I'll stick to the trail, thank you."

"Trust me. I'd rather have someone else do it for me, too. But it's the only way my dad will let me go. He's been making me earn survival patches every weekend for months." George took a stack of homemade patches from a side pocket of his backpack. "Making a fire without matches, finding water, identifying poisonous and edible plants," George said, tossing the makeshift patches on a pile. The fire patch looked like it had been cut from a barbecue apron. "He wasn't going to let me go if I didn't earn them all," George said, throwing the rest of the homemade patches on the pile. "And since this is the first year we'll get to stay in the upper field with the big kids, there was no way I was going to miss out. I'll finally be rid of my little sister always tagging along at my heels down at the Kiddie Cabins."

At summer camp, everyone coveted sleeping out under the stars in the lean-tos in the upper field about a half a mile from the main cabins. But they were only for middle-schoolers. Kids graduated from the cabins to the lean-tos during the summer between fifth and sixth grades. It was like a Camp Calamity rite of passage.

"What's next on the list?" George asked.

"Uh, a hatchet."

"Ah." George smiled. He went to the garage and brought out a brand-new hatchet in a tanned-leather case. "My dad gave me this for earning my last patch: survival shelters." He removed the hatchet from its case. The silver-edged blade gleamed in the sun. "Isn't it awesome?"

Abby wrinkled her brow. "Looks dangerous."

George shuffled through the patches until he found the one that read: *Gear Safety*. "That was what this patch was for."

Just then Peter and John shuffled up the driveway. Peter's untied sneaker laces slapped him in the shins as he walked.

"Hey guys, whatcha doing?" Peter asked.

"What's it look like they're doing, having a tea party?" John said, cutting George off as he was about to answer. "Let's take a cue from Arthur Conan Doyle's famous sleuth Sherlock Holmes and make a deduction: Abby's holding a clipboard with a checklist on it, George has his well-used camping gear spread out on the driveway, and our yearly trip to Camp Calamity is less than a week away—it's elementary my dear Peter! They're picking boogers!" John chuckled at his own joke.

"Ha, ha, very funny," Peter said, clearly not in the mood for jokes. "Maybe it was a stupid question, but it was more a figure of speech— you know, to break the ice."

"I know. I's just raggin' on ya," John said, still chuckling.

Peter's expression turned serious. "But, uhm, seriously guys, what *are* you doing?" He gave John an awkward glance.

"Oh yeah, that's right," John said, finally coming around to what Peter was getting at. "Didn't ya hear?"

"Hear what?" Abby asked. She held the pencil to her mouth.

"They're talking about closing the camp for the rest of the summer."

"Closing the camp!"

"The counselors are meeting today."

"Oh, no," George said, slumping to his knees. "I've waited all year for this. I've been working towards it for months!"

"They said they're going to make a decision by the end of the day," Peter said.

"I was so looking forward to sleeping out in the lean-tos this year, and staying up late with the big kids," George said, letting his frustration show, "not to mention getting away from my little sister for a change."

"Kylie's not so bad," Peter said, trying to cheer him up. John gave Peter an odd look. Peter shrugged.

"I can't believe it," George said, clearly discouraged as he looked over his gear.

"Well, they said they're just not sure," John said, "not with everything that's been going on."

"What do you mean?" Abby asked.

"It may just be too dangerous."

"Dangerous?" Abby's eyes grew wide, and her body stiffened. They had her complete attention.

"I heard things had gotten a little weird out at the camp lately, but I didn't think it was that serious," George replied.

"Well, sometimes little things tend to add up," John said.

"And a lot of little weird things can sometimes make one great big mystery," Peter added.

"What mystery?" Abby asked.

"Something strange is going on at the camp. Everyone seems to be on edge right now," John said, "especially after what happened last night."

"What happened?" Abby said, growing impatient.

"Didn't you hear the news?"

2.

GEORGE AND Abby stood motionless in the driveway, hovering over George's camping gear and wondering if they'd get a chance to use it this year. John and Peter had stopped by. Now it seemed their yearly summer trip to Camp Calamity was in jeopardy.

"What happened?" George asked.

"Mrs. Nussbaum's cat has gone missing," John said.

"Oh, no," Abby said, "not Jeepers." Jeepers was their old third-grade teacher's cat. It had been kind of like their class mascot—even though Emily Davison was sort of allergic and sort of started sneezing whenever it was around.

"Yeah, Jeepers."

"That cat is crazy," George said. "I've never seen it walk. It's always scrambling around all over the place."

"Well, it's the fifth cat that's gone missing in the last month," Peter said. "All of them lived close to the woods near Camp Calamity."

"It's probably just hunting mice in the Davison's barn again."

"That's part of the problem," John said. "There's been trouble at Davison's farm, too. They're missing six chickens from their coop."

"Six chickens?"

"Yep, nothing left but a bunch of feathers."

"I heard the Albertson's dog has gone missing, too," Peter said. "But they live all the way over on the other end of town, so it may have just run away."

"Wait a minute," Abby said. "What's all of this got to do with summer camp?"

John and Peter gave each other a concerned look. Then they looked at George. John raised his eyebrow.

"No way," George said, reading their minds, "you can't be serious."

"Yep."

"That's an old wive's tale, a story they tell little kids to scare them."

"What story?" Abby asked.

"The Calamity Hollow Howler."

"The Hollow Howler?" Abby said doubtfully. "I haven't heard that story in like forever, since my first summer in the Camp Calamity Kiddie Cabins."

"My neighbor, Timothy Arnold, told me that campers have heard strange sounds coming from the woods every night for the past month," Peter said, "awful sounds, like animals crunching on bones."

"They've heard grunting and growling, too—and howling coming from the direction of the ravine," John added.

"The ravine?" Abby asked.

"You know, Calamity Hollow. Even the grown-ups have heard it."

"Still," Abby said, not yet convinced, "the Hollow Howler? I thought the counselors told that story to keep the kids away from the Hollow."

"My dad told me it was true," Peter said. "That's how the camp got its name. Years ago, a kid went missing and wandered into the ravine. They say that the Howler got him and he was never heard from again. That's when they named it Calamity Hollow."

"There's got to be another explanation, though," Abby said. "For the cats disappearing, I mean."

"Maybe it's a wolf or a mountain lion," George said, wondering aloud. "They've been known to show up around here once in a while."

"Well, something has the counselors spooked," Peter replied, looking grim. Spooked. It seemed unthinkable, but it was true. The counselors were worried, worried enough to close the camp. The thought hung over them like a dark cloud. Could it really be the Howler?

"Let's look at this scientifically," John said. "The only hard evidence we have is that these animals have gone missing. Everything else is just rumors."

"Well, whatever it is," George said, repacking his backpack, "it's enough to make them want to close Camp Calamity and keep us away from summer camp this year. And they've never done that before. All of our plans will be ruined."

"We'll just have to wait and see what happens," John replied.

* * *

That night at dinner, George picked at his food. He had lost his appetite. He moved his peas and mashed potatoes around with his fork to make it look like he had eaten something. He snuck some pieces off his plate and gave them to his dog Buster when he thought no one else was looking. He sat there looking glum. Kylie was having a great time, though, which somehow made him feel even grumpier. It was her favorite meal: chicken fingers and apple sauce. Even though she was going into second grade, she still loved piling the potatoes up like a mountain and pouring the peas down the side. She laughed as she plunged a chicken finger into the mush and scooped everything up together. George's mom chuckled as Kylie took a big bite. She wiped Kylie's mouth with a napkin. George's dad gave Kylie a questioning look.

"She's fine, dear," George's mom said, reassuring him, "I'm just happy she's eating."

George's dad smiled.

George turned his back toward his sister and propped his head up with his hand. How could she be so happy when their summer camping trip was in jeopardy? George's dad noticed George shuffling his food around.

"What's the matter, sport?" his dad said.

"Nothing."

"Awe, come on, now," he said. "Something's the matter. I can always tell when something's bothering you."

"How?"

"Well, Buster's happier, for one." Buster sat there, wagging his tail and licking his lips.

"I guess I'm just upset about summer camp."

"Uh-huh. Well, they haven't decided anything yet, or we would have heard something."

"How about I call over there after dinner," Mom said, "to see if they've made up their minds yet. How would that be?"

George nodded. It made him feel a little better. Not knowing only made it worse. Kylie tossed some peas down her potato mountain. They tumbled to the floor. Buster scurried over and gobbled them up.

"Yea, Buster!" Kylie squealed.

"Hey, Dad?" George said.

"Yeah?"

"You went to summer camp at Camp Calamity when you were a kid, too, right?"

"You better believe I did. I can remember my first year in the upper field. They didn't have those nice lean-tos like they do now. We had to build our own, which was much more fun if you ask me. You're sleeping in style, now."

"Do you believe in the Hollow Howler?"

George's dad smirked. "Well," he said in a sing-song voice and shifted around in his seat like he was getting ready to tell one of his long stories.

"Donald," George's mom said, in her warning voice. She always used full names when she meant business—even with George's dad.

"Well, George," he said, in a more serious tone, clearly bummed he wouldn't get to tell his story, but glad he wouldn't have to face his wife's wrath. "That story has been around for a long time, and it always seems to pop up this time of year, when the kids are getting ready for summer camp. But I think it's just a story they tell to scare the kids."

"And keep them away from Calamity Hollow?"

"Yes, that's right, to keep the kids away from Calamity Hollow. That ravine can be very dangerous if you don't know what you're doing."

George was satisfied with his dad's answer. Then he thought about the missing cats.

"What about the pets that have gone missing—and the Davison's chickens? There has to be some explanation."

"Well, that's true, George. It could be a bear or a mountain lion—or it could just be a coincidence. These things happen."

"I hope they don't close the camp for the summer."

"Sometimes you have to err on the side of caution—you know that, from the patches you've earned. You can never be too cautious."

That's when the phone rang. George's mother got up to answer it.

"Hello?" George's mother answered from the hall.

It was Mr. Jensen, Camp Calamity's director.

3.

"YES, MR. Jensen," George's mom said, speaking into the phone. "I think that's the smartest thing to do." George's heart sank.
"Oh no," he whispered, dropping his head to his chest.

"Thank you, Mr. Jensen," George's mom continued. "I'll tell them. I'm sure it's probably for the best." She hung up the phone and came back to the table. Everyone waited for her to say something, even Buster, although he probably hoped it would be about table scraps.

George frowned, preparing himself for the news.

"Well?" George's dad said. "What's the verdict?"

George looked at his mom's face, but he couldn't read her. She had the best poker face. All moms did.

"Well, Mom? What'd he say?"

"He apologized for taking so long to call, but he said they had gone back and forth for hours trying to make a decision."

"And?"

"And they've decided to keep the camp open."

"All right!" George yelled, pushing the chair back from the table. It was as if his mom had just let go of a half-inflated balloon.

"Yea, Buster!" Kylie said, clearly not paying attention.

"No, Kylie," George said, feeling like a good big brother again. "We're going to summer camp!"

"Oh," Kylie said. "I thought we were already going?"

"Yeah, but they had almost canceled it."

"Oh, oops! Yea, summer camp!" She held up a chicken finger in a victory salute. Everyone laughed.

"But," George's mom said, turning serious again.

"But? But what?"

"But they said there are going to be some extra rules and some changes."

"That's probably smart," George's dad said.

"Extra rules?" George asked, sounding a little deflated. Rules were never fun to begin with—and *extra* rules seemed more like a punishment. "Like what?"

George's mom glanced at his dad. "Well, I think you'll just have to wait and see." She wasn't telling him something. George was sure of it.

"Awe come on, mom."

"Oh, yes," George's dad said, coming to her rescue. "I think that would be a good idea. You'll have to wait and see. You can't do anything about it, so why worry?" George couldn't argue. The logic was sound, so he let it go. "But this is good news for you, right, George?" his father continued. "Your trip is saved! You're going to have so much fun. Fishing, canoeing, swimming . . . and you'll finally be with the big kids."

His dad was right. The crisis had been averted. Things were looking up. The trip was back on.

4.

THE FOLLOWING morning, George tucked the list of things he needed to buy at the store into his front pocket and headed out the door. It was rare that his mother would let him walk the six blocks into town alone, so he was thrilled when she suggested he could go to Walter's Hardware Store to pick up the supplies that he needed. Going into middle school had its advantages.

Since it always made sense to use the buddy system (he learned that while earning his second patch: *Survival Readiness)*, he planned to meet Abby at the end of the driveway.

"Hey, Abby," he said when he saw her. "Good news, huh? About Camp Calamity?"

"Yeah, looks like you'll get to use that new gear after all."

The two of them started down the street. "Yeah. Thanks for helping me organize it. Would you mind helping me finish the checklist later? We kind of got sidetracked yesterday."

"You mean interrupted by John and Peter and their wild imaginations."

"So you think there's nothing to worry about? About the Howler, I mean."

"Well, I wouldn't say that. It's just, there has to be some reason those cats have gone missing."

"Don't forget about the Davison's chickens."

"Right. I'm not convinced there's some big boogie man hiding in the woods."

"I guess you're probably right. It is strange, though. You know, all those weird noises the campers have heard—and what about that kid who went missing."

"You mean when the camp first opened?"

"Yeah."

"There's no evidence that the Howler got him. He probably just got lost or hurt or something because he was somewhere he wasn't supposed to be."

"You mean like in the Hollow."

"Yeah. That place can be dangerous. There are cliffs and rockslides and sinkholes—at least that's what my parents have said. I've never seen it. I always stick to the trail."

"Yeah, you're probably right."

They were almost halfway to Walter's Hardware Store. John's house was right around the corner. They took a detour when they saw him and Peter shooting hoops in the driveway.

"Hey guys," George said. "Whatcha doing?" He regretted saying it as soon as it came out of his mouth. He realized what was coming before he even finished the question. Abby rolled her eyes.

"Let's see," John said, smiling. "An orange basketball, an eight-foot hoop, tally marks on the driveway . . . we're picking boogers!"

"Ha, ha, very funny. You got to come up with a new line, though."

"Yeah, that one's getting old," Abby agreed.

"Okay, okay," John said, still smiling.

"You guys wanna go with us to Walter's? My mom gave me some money to pick up some of the gear I need for the trip."

"Yeah, sure! That sounds great," John said, tossing the basketball into the yard. "Let me go ask my mom and get some money for a soda." John's mom and dad were a little less strict than George's. He thought it might be because John lived closer to town, but he wasn't sure. The wooden screen door slapped when John returned. "She says it's okay. We just have to be back in an hour."

"No problem," George said.

The four of them headed toward town.

Old-timers liked to hang out at Walter's Hardware Store to gossip and drink coffee. Kids, however, were drawn to the penny candy jars on the counter and the soda machines out back. Parents felt safe letting their kids go there because Sheriff Brown and his deputies liked to hang out there, too.

When they got there, George divided his list between the four of them, and they spread out across the store. The narrow wooden floorboards creaked under their feet as they searched the aisles for rope, batteries, fishhooks, and waterproof matches.

Peter and George hurdled up the stairs, two-by-two, heading for the camping gear on the second level. When they reached the aisle overlooking the counter, Peter overheard Sheriff Brown talking to Mr. Walter, who was standing behind the cash register.

"It's just so strange what's going on out there," Sheriff Brown said. "First cats, then chickens, and now this."

Peter's eyes widened. He smiled as if he had just overheard his mom telling his dad where she hid the Christmas presents. He motioned for George to come closer to the railing.

"It's awfully eerie if you ask me," Mr. Walter replied.

George's jaw dropped. He knew they shouldn't be eavesdropping. He shook his head and started to leave. Peter grabbed his arm and pleaded with him silently to stay. George caved.

"Well, the cats and chickens I can understand," the sheriff said. "I'm sure they make for a tasty treat for some mountain lion or wolf— or maybe even a hawk or something. But this?"

Abby and John appeared at the top of the stairs. Peter motioned for them wildly. They walked over, looking puzzled. Peter pressed his finger to his lips and pointed to the sheriff standing below.

"I can't make heads nor tails of it," Sheriff Brown said. "But, you're right. When I think about it, it does kind of give me the creeps."

"Are you going to notify the public?"

"No, not just yet. I don't want anyone to panic."

"What about Camp Calamity?"

"I spoke with Mr. Jensen, the camp director, last night, and he's pretty confident with the measures they have in place. They're used to wild animals wandering around. It's common to see bears and what not around there every once in a while. The counselors are trained on how to handle them. They tie up the garbage and make themselves known when hiking in the woods. They'll make sure the kids are safe."

"Bears and mountain lions are one thing sheriff, but this? I've been hunting them woods out there around the camp all my life, and I've never seen a bear do something like that to that deer." Mr. Walter lowered his voice until it was almost at a whisper. "I mean, that thing was ripped to shreds and hardly even eaten. No animal I've come across would waste a meal like that. It was like it did it just for fun."

Abby grabbed the two boys standing next to her, contorting her face in a huge grimace. John put his hand on his stomach and pretended like he was going to puke. Peter shook his head and pressed his finger to his lips, pleading with them to be quiet.

"Well, I would have to agree. It's odd, but you don't know what happened out there. That bear or wolf or whatever it was could've gotten spooked before it had a chance to eat, which is probably why it killed the goat, too. It was still hungry."

"But it didn't eat the goat either." Sheriff Brown didn't respond. Everything was silent for a moment. Mr. Walter continued, "chickens and cats now a deer and a goat; the animals keep getting bigger, don't they?"

A customer came to the counter, and Sheriff Brown ended the conversation.

"I'll catch you later, Walt," the sheriff said, "I've got to head out to the Davison's to take a statement."

"Yeah, see ya later, Brownie."

The four kids moved to the top of the stairs.

"Did you hear . . . ?" Peter whispered.

George shook his head and put his hand over Peter's mouth. "Not here, you goober! If they realize we heard 'em, they'll close the camp for sure! Our summer will be ruined!"

"He's right," John whispered.

"You guys sneak down the stairs and out the back. I'll wait a few minutes then take my stuff to the counter. When I'm done, I'll meet you around back."

George wandered around the store until Mr. Walter went into the office. When the stock boy took over the register, George took his things to the counter. He paid, grabbed his bag, and sprinted out the front door. He took a hard left and cut around the side. When he reached the back, he ran straight into Seth Logan and Jerry Magee, two of the biggest bullies in school, whom he always tried to avoid at all costs.

5.

IN THE back of Walter's Hardware Store, away from prying eyes, Seth Logan had his hands clasped behind John's head in a wrestling move called a full nelson. John's arms splayed out to the sides, so he kind of looked like a plucked chicken held up by the wings. Jerry Magee had Peter in a headlock and was grinding into his temple with his knuckles. Abby, however, was ready to pounce. She stood with her hands on her hips, scolding the bullies unmercifully.

"You two snot-sucking hamsters don't have enough brains to understand this," Abby warned, "but I'm giving you to the count of ten to let go of them before I knock your teeth out!"

Now George had seen Abby get angry before. He had been on the receiving end of that anger one too many times than he liked to remember. If there was anything he dreaded more than running into Seth and Jerry, it was being around Abby Turner when she got angry.

Abby had a large vocabulary and a sharp brain. She could persuade you to see things her way so fast you couldn't remember why you had disagreed with her in the first place. She was also a second-degree red belt in Taekwondo, so no one ever dared to try to bully her. There were many times in George's life that he was glad that Abby had been his best friend since preschool. Now was one of those times.

Seth and Jerry had eased up on their victims a bit, unsure of what to make of the four-foot-tall fireball in front of them. The balance of power shifted considerably in Abby's favor when George bounded around the corner and ran into the two ruffians.

"George! Am I glad to see you." Abby said, "Which one do you want: the toilet-drinker or the pimple-licker?"

"You better watch yourself, Georgie," Seth warned.

"Yeah, George," Jerry chimed in, "don't do anything stupid. Your girlfriend won't always be around to protect you."

Between the four of them, they outnumbered Seth and Jerry, but that didn't mean they had won. A cornered animal is often the most dangerous. He had to give them a way out. "Hey, why don't you let them go, guys," George said, trying to sound neutral. "I just saw Sheriff Brown out front. You wouldn't want him to catch you fighting again, would you?"

George could almost see the hamster wheel spinning in Seth's head.

"You know what? I'm getting bored pulling the wings off little fifth-graders," Seth said, releasing John from the wrestling hold.

"Yeah, they're all nerd burgers. That's for sure," Jerry said, pushing Peter to the ground.

"They don't have long to live anyway, right, Jer?"

George helped Peter to his feet.

"Yeah, you'll all be Howler food soon," Jerry taunted. "Didn't ya hear? The Hollow Howler is back, and it's ready to exact its revenge."

"You'll be sorry," Seth said. "Its victims are getting bigger—no more chickens and cats, now it's a deer and a goat. It's just getting ready for you! By the time you get to Camp Calamity, it'll be hungry for something say . . . kid-sized!"

"Why don't you shut-up and eat boogers, you pimple pinchers!" Abby said.

"Come on, Abby," Peter said, trying to separate them. "Let's get out of here."

George and his friends made their way to the side of the building, making sure they kept a sharp eye on the retreating Seth and Jerry.

"So long losers!" Seth yelled from a distance, trying to get in the last word. "Have a nice life, what's left of it!"

John massaged his arm while Peter rubbed the brush burn on his temple.

"Are you guys all right?" George asked as they rounded the front of the building.

"Yeah, nothing we haven't dealt with before," John said, scowling.

"Don't worry about them," Peter said, trying to cheer him up. "Those guys are lowlifes." John nodded. "What happened anyway?"

"They ambushed us as we came out the back door," Peter replied.

"They must have been spying on us," John said.

"Yeah, they knew everything we were doing, buying supplies for Camp Calamity and all."

"And did you hear? They even knew about the Howler!"

"Yeah, and that it's moved on from chickens and cats to larger animals, so they must have heard the sheriff and Mr. Walter talking, too."

"I can't believe the sheriff's not going to tell anyone. People have to know that there's a monster on the loose."

"Wait a minute," Abby said, stopping everyone in their tracks. "You're not telling me you guys actually believe in this Howler do you?"

"You heard what Mr. Walter said, right?" Peter said, pointing back toward the hardware store. "Those animals were half eaten!"

"No, the sheriff said that they hadn't been eaten at all," George replied, correcting him, "just ripped to shreds."

"Well, what else could it be?" Peter asked.

"Maybe it's a wolf."

"Could be a bear."

"A mountain lion—definitely could be a mountain lion."

The four of them started walking again.

"Or," John said, "it could be a cryptid."

"What's a cryptid?" George asked.

"Cryptozoology is the study of creatures whose existence hasn't been proven yet. A creature that has yet to be discovered is called a cryptid."

"You mean like Bigfoot or the Loch Ness Monster?"

"Something like that."

"Those things don't exist," Abby said.

"Well, giant squids and sea serpents were once thought to be myths until the late nineteenth or early twentieth centuries," John said, "and Komodo dragons weren't proven to be real until the 1920s. No one believed mountain gorillas existed either."

"What if we could solve the mystery," Peter said, dreaming. "What if we could prove the Howler is real? We'd be famous!"

"That's a tall order. No one has been able to prove it so far," John said.

"But has anyone ever tried?"

No one could think of anyone. They could only remember stories of people who had claimed to have seen it, and even those were rumors not firsthand accounts.

"We would have to find evidence," John said.

"No one is going to believe a bunch of kids," Abby said.

"That's why we'd have to find solid proof or no one will believe us."

"Wait a minute," George said, stopping everyone again. "What are we talking about here? Are we actually talking about going out to look for the Howler?" No one spoke. They were all mulling the idea over in their heads. It seemed ridiculous, perhaps even deadly, but it intrigued them.

"Well," Abby said, "the evidence might prove what's killing those animals is actually something else, not the Howler. Either way, we'd solve the mystery."

"Okay, I guess I see your point," George said, still not quite convinced. "But what if we found it? What if we went out looking for evidence and we actually *ran into the Howler?*"

The question hung in the air like a stench. No one wanted to go near it.

"I think it's unlikely," Abby said, breaking the silence. "But something is ripping those animals apart. We'd have to be careful. We'd have to be ready."

6.

THAT NIGHT after dinner, George's father asked him to take Buster for his evening walk. Normally, George would have complained, but tonight he thought it sounded like a good idea. He had a lot on his mind, and a walk always helped him unwind. Besides, he needed a break from organizing his camping gear.

George reached up and unhitched Buster's leash from its hook next to the door and fastened it to Buster's collar. The night was sticky and warm, so he hurried to get out of the humid garage. Outside, clouds hid the canopy of stars overhead. When they reached the edge of the driveway, the darkness pressed in on them, and George noticed he couldn't see the Furgesons' house at the end of the street. He could just see past his next-door neighbors, the O'Rileys.

George followed behind Buster, retracing the steps of their typical route: left out of the driveway in the opposite direction of town, past the O'Rileys', the Driscolls', and the Furgesons', and onto the jogging path that led to the woods. Buster made his usual stops along the route, sniffing every mailbox to see which of his doggie buddies had been there before him.

As they walked, George couldn't help but remember the conversation he had overheard earlier in the day, and it made him uneasy. Only yesterday, the counselors had called a meeting because they were worried about the recent animal disappearances and all the strange things that had been going on in the woods around Camp Calamity. In short, they were spooked. Now it seemed clear that Sheriff Brown and Mr. Walter were, too—and, despite Peter and John's excitement, and Abby's careful logic, George wasn't sure if going out to look for the Howler was a good idea.

George prided himself with being prepared, and whether it was the Howler or some yet to be discovered creature, something was killing those animals. The question was, what? How can you prepare yourself for something if you don't know what it is? Was he afraid? He didn't know. He only knew he was worried. But he couldn't decide whether he was worried about not being prepared or about running into the Howler, and that bothered him. Perhaps it was both, he decided. Maybe he was worried about not being prepared if they ran into the Howler.

Buster tugged on the leash. His nose seemed overly active tonight. He sniffed the edges of the flowerbeds and between the shrubbery lining the sidewalk. He seemed to be on to something, tracking a particular scent. It pulled him along by his nose, which was glued to the ground like a bloodhound's. He darted back and forth, tugging the leash this way and that.

"What's the matter, Buster?" George said, somewhat annoyed that his relaxing walk had turned tense. They stepped off the sidewalk and onto the jogging path.

Buster froze. He lifted his head and stared into the dark woods ahead. Then he growled and let out a small woof under his breath. George squinted against the darkness, trying to decipher the black blurry shapes in front of him. He felt cold. It wasn't a physical cold, like a chill breeze that blows on a winter's night. It was a nervous cold, like a subconscious shiver that comes from the primordial recesses of your mind. His thoughts turned to the Howler and to what Mr. Walter had said about the deer being ripped apart. He tried to push the thought out of his mind, but it was no use. His fear had gotten the best of him.

"What is it, Buster?" George's voice broke halfway through the question. He gulped. He heard a faint rustling sound coming from somewhere in the woods, or did he? He wasn't sure. Buster's ears twitched, and George strained to listen again. Nothing.

"Come on, Buster," George said, pulling him in the opposite direction, "let's go back."

Then George heard the unmistakable cracking of branches and shuffling of dry leaves of someone—or some*thing*—trudging through the woods. Buster let out several loud and sharp barks, startling George and making his heart race.

"It's okay, Buster," George said, though not quite convinced himself.

Buster lunged forward and whipped the leash out of George's hand. George flailed for it as Buster took off down the path dragging the leash behind him.

"No! Buster come! Come!"

George watched helplessly as Buster pulled away and disappeared into the woods.

"Buster! Buster!"

George ran after his fleeing pet but stopped a few feet shy of the tree line. Buster's frantic bark echoed somewhere in the distance. Then there was a high-pitched yelp, and the barking stopped. The woods became stone silent.

7.

GEORGE STOOD on the jogging path, just feet away from where it entered the woods and was swallowed up by the darkness. Buster, his beloved dog, had gotten away from him. A few hours before, Buster had sat wagging his tail as he begged for food at the dinner table. Now he had gone missing, just like Mrs. Nussbaum's cat, the Albertson's dog, and the Davison's chickens. One minute he was there, happily sniffing the flowerbeds that framed the mailboxes along the sidewalk. In the next moment, he was gone, vanishing in a flurry of barks that ended in a high-pitched yelp somewhere in the dark woods.

For a short time, a strange sort of silence fell over the neighborhood. But now the night sounds had returned, and George stood alone on the jogging path, listening to the buzzing katydids and the chirping crickets. What would he tell his mom and dad? Buster had been his responsibility. He shuddered at the thought of Buster lying somewhere in the woods, and in his mind, the horrible images of the Davison's goat, lying on the ground in bloodied pieces, were replaced with a similar image of Buster.

George felt sick. He leaned over and thought he'd puke. Then he heard footfalls coming down the path from the direction of the woods. He could swear he heard Buster's toenails tapping out their usual trot along with them.

He peered into the woods and noticed shadows move along the path. All at once, he saw Buster scampering toward him happily wagging his tail. For a moment, George thought he was seeing things. Then he saw his neighbor, Mr. Furgeson, dressed in a fluorescent green running vest, following not far behind with Buster's leash looped in his hand.

"George? Is that you?" He said. "Are you all right?"

Not only was Mr. Furgeson George's neighbor, but he was also his mailman, and he was probably Buster's best friend in the whole neighborhood. Mr. Furgeson always carried doggie treats in his pocket, most mail carriers did, and he always had a special one just for Buster.

"Uh, yeah, Mr. Furgeson, thanks."

"Are you sure? You look a little sick, there."

"Uh, yeah, I'm okay, really. I just got a little overheated."

"Yeah, I know what you mean. I had to cut my nightly run a little short tonight." He handed Buster's leash to George. "Looks like Buster got away from you. Sorry, I think I stepped on his tail when he ran up to me. It's so dark I didn't see him coming until he was right in front of me!"

"That's okay. Thanks, Mr. Furgeson."

"No problem, George." Mr. Furgeson started down the path, heading toward his house.

"Uh, Mr. Furgeson?" George said, catching him before he ran off.

"Yes, George?"

"You didn't see anything uh . . . strange out there in the woods, did you?"

"Strange? Like what?"

"Oh, I don't know. Like an animal or something? I thought I heard something before Buster ran off."

"No, George, can't say that I did, save for the usual rabbits and squirrels."

George looked into the woods, scanning the shadows. "Oh, okay."

"Are you sure you're all right, George?"

"Yeah, Mr. Furgeson. I'm fine. Thanks for catching Buster for me."

"No problem, George. You head straight home now," Mr. Furgeson said, wrinkling his brow. "I'm a little worried about you."

"Okay, Mr. F."

Mr. Furgeson jogged down the path and onto the sidewalk.

"Come on, Buster, you big dummy," George said. "Let's go home. I've had enough walking for one night."

George and Buster made their way down the path, heading back in the direction they had come. When they had almost reached the sidewalk, the katydids and crickets ceased, and the woods became silent again. George turned and looked over his shoulder in the direction of the woods. He could have sworn he saw a dark figure slip across the jogging path.

8.

IT WAS the day before they were scheduled to leave for summer camp, and George, Peter, John, and Abby had planned to meet in John's backyard treehouse to take stock of the supplies that they had gathered for their mission. They needed a place where they could meet in secret. If their parents or any other grown-up found out what they were planning, that they were going out searching for the Howler, they'd be in deep trouble, and their yearly trip to Camp Calamity would be in jeopardy, too. John's treehouse seemed like the perfect location. It sat in the tree line away from the house, and in the canopy of leaves, it was well out of sight of the road.

George arrived first, taking the shortcut in between the houses, being careful to avoid being seen by prying eyes along the way. It was pretty much a straight shot as the crow flies between George's house and John's. He could almost see the roof of John's house three blocks away when he looked out his second-floor bathroom window.

George cut around to the back of John's house, skipping the customary courtesy of ringing the front doorbell, and climbed the ladder to the treehouse. John had his gear spread out over the floor, waiting for them when George arrived.

"Did you get the binoculars?" John asked before George even got through the trapdoor in the floor.

"Yes, John. Relax."

"Are you sure your dad won't know you took them?"

"Don't worry. He never uses them anymore. He won't even realize they're missing."

George unbuckled his backpack, which was newly adorned with his eighteen survival patches that his dad had sewn on the previous night.

"Hey, I like your patches," John said.

"Thanks," George replied, trying not to roll his eyes. He was so sick of his dad making him earn those patches. But he guessed they did look pretty impressive, now that he thought about it. He dumped the contents of his backpack onto the wooden floor along with John's supplies, and the two of them started sorting it when Abby and Peter arrived.

"Hey, nice patches," Peter said, noticing them right away. That kid never missed anything.

"Thanks."

"Did you bring the game camera?" John asked Peter, barely able to contain himself.

Peter unzipped his bag and slowly removed a brand new, camouflaged game camera, still in the box. It was almost like he was removing an antique vase or something.

"Wow," John said, almost singing. "That thing looks awesome!"

"What's a game camera?" Abby asked.

"It's a motion-activated digital camera inside a waterproof case. It's used to track animals. You strap the box onto a tree or something, turn it on, and leave. If an animal walks by, it'll snap its picture. Then you can come back later to see if you got anything."

"That is pretty cool," Abby said.

"Where did you get that thing?" George asked.

"In my dad's hunting gear," Peter said. "He bought a new one at the end of the season last year when his busted, so he never got a chance to use it. He won't go looking for it until deer season next fall."

"Awesome," George replied.

"I also bought a disposable camera from Walter's with my birthday money," Peter said, handing George a yellow plastic camera.

"What do you got, Abby?"

Abby unloaded her bag, which was more like a large purse. "Let's see: specimen bottles, collection baggies, latex gloves, a black marker—oh and tweezers."

"Where did you get all of that stuff?"

"From my insect collecting kit."

"The Howler's a *huge beast,* you idiot, not a bug!" Peter said, taking his life into his hands, calling Abby an idiot. "Why would you bring *tweezers?*"

"Let's make a deduction," John said, mocking Peter. "First, Abby's probably the smartest kid here. Second, she has surmised by the animals that the Howler has killed that it's probably pretty big. Third, she knows we're trying to collect evidence to prove it actually exists."

"Or that it doesn't exist," Abby interjected.

"Right. Last, she knows that the evidence we find could be small, like bits of hair, fingernails, skin, or teeth, so why did she bring the tweezers? For picking boogers!"

Everyone moaned except John. The joke had clearly gotten old.

"Okay, fair enough," Peter said.

"Now that everyone's here, let's see what we've got," John said. "Along with the stuff you guys brought, we have four flashlights, two bear whistles, some waterproof matches, flint, and a pocketknife."

"I also bought a map of the county that includes Camp Calamity and the surrounding woods, oh and a compass," George said, taking them out of his backpack.

"And I've got my new paracord survival bracelet," Peter said, holding out his wrist. "The army uses it to hold parachutes. It's got a 550-pound break strength!"

"Okay. What do we have to protect ourselves with? I have my pocketknife."

"I've got my hatchet," George said. "I was planning to bring it anyway."

"I'll grab my brother's slingshot. He won't care," Peter said. "I'll smuggle it out in my sleeping bag, just in case."

"How about you, Abby?"

"Are you kidding?" Peter said. "Her whole body's a lethal weapon."

"Well, she has to have something."

"I'll bring along my mother's pepper spray," Abby said. "She used to carry it when she ran in the park, but now she just goes to the gym."

"Okay, sounds like a plan."

"Is everyone sure about this?" George said. "I mean, besides trying to track a deadly animal, it'll be extremely dangerous out there in that hollow."

"Not to mention we risk getting ourselves into serious trouble with the camp counselors—and our parents," Abby added.

"Well, I'm in," Peter said. "I've wanted to do something like this my whole life." He held his fist out over their gear. "Who's with me?"

"I am," John said, slapping his hand on top of Peter's. "We could go down in history for finding a cryptid! We'll be famous!"

"I am, too," Abby said, laying her hand on John's. "I want to be there to see your faces when you guys are proven wrong. That'll be priceless."

They all looked at George, who sat there staring at them.

"Well, what'd you say, George?" John said. "Are you in?"

George looked each of them in the eye.

"How 'bout it, George?" Abby said, smiling.

"Someone's got to be there to get you guys out of a mess if you get yourselves in trouble." He slapped his hand on top of Abby's. "I'm in."

Each of them added their other hands to the pile. The game was on.

9.

THE FIRST day of summer camp was more liked controlled chaos. Camp Calamity called it "move-in day," but to George and his friends it was affectionately known as "mayhem day." You could always count on at least one newbie getting lost or ending up in the wrong cabin on the first day. But this was George's fifth summer at Camp Calamity, and he wasn't worried. For the past few years, he had navigated through the check-in process like a pro.

George and his family drove through the gates at 7:30 a.m. sharp. "Might as well get used to getting up with the sun," his father had said. The Camp Director, Mr. Jensen, greeted them at the gate.

"Good Morning!" Mr. Jensen said as George's dad rolled down the window. "We're going to do things a little differently this year, so we're asking all the campers to take all their gear and meet us in the Calamity Canteen."

"Calamity Canteen?" George said, wondering out loud. "Why are we meeting in the Canteen?"

The Calamity Canteen was the camp's main dining hall. Most of the time, George and his friends cooked their meals around the campfire, but the dining hall was great for when they got too busy or didn't feel like cooking.

"Well, I told you, George, that there are going to be some changes this year—and some extra rules," George's mom said, turning around from the front seat. "They probably just want to tell everyone at the same time." She turned back toward the front. As she did, George noticed her give his dad an odd look. It was the same look she had given him at dinner a few nights earlier when Mr. Jensen called and told them their decision about the camp.

"Mom, what?"

"Never mind, George," his mom said.

"So there is something you're not telling me."

George's mom looked at his dad again. He shook his head, and his mother nodded.

"Mom, Dad, what is it you're not telling me?"

"You'll just have to wait and see, George," his mom said, not bothering to turn around. "I'm sure both you and Kylie are going to have a great time."

George grabbed his sleeping bag, backpack, and duffel bag from the trunk of the car. The gear for their secret mission was hidden in his backpack. He slipped it over his shoulders right away, just to be sure it wouldn't end up in the wrong hands. Then he grabbed his sister Kylie's suitcase and sleeping bag, too. They were a matching pink set with pictures of cartoon ponies on them. Kylie didn't need as much gear as George did since she'd be staying in the Kitty Cabins.

"Have fun!" George's dad said. "Watch out for the poison ivy."

"Okay, Dad."

"And please check on your sister once in a while. Okay, George?"

"Yes, mom," George said, rolling his eyes. He really didn't mind checking on her, but he had to play the part of the annoyed big brother.

"We love you, honey," his mom said, leaning over to kiss him. "Help your sister get where she's going, will you?"

"Okay, mom."

"Have fun, sport," his dad said.

George and Kylie made their way toward the Canteen, which was down the path on the other side of the main lodge. When they got to the lodge, Peter and John were waiting for them on the steps.

"Hey, George!" Peter yelled. "We saw you coming!"

"Hey Peter, John," George said when he got closer, "When'd you get here?"

"About ten minutes ago," Peter said. "My mom forgot to buy my nose strips, so we had to leave early to get some."

"Nose strips?"

"I can't sleep without them. I get all stuffed up and can't breathe!"

"Better than picking boogers," John said, laughing.

"Shut up," Peter said.

Abby walked up from the parking lot.

"Hey, guys," Abby said. "Does everyone have their gear—you know, for the mission?"

George and John nodded.

"Smuggled it out with no problem," Peter said, tapping his sleeping bag.

"Does anyone know what this meeting's about?" George asked.

Everyone shook their heads.

"My mom said it's something about sleeping arrangements," Peter said.

"Sleeping arrangements?"

"Hey! Give it back!" someone yelled from nearby.

George looked around. "Wait—where's Kylie?"

"Oh, no," John said, massaging his arm and looking the other way. "Huh?"

"There," Peter said, pointing down the path and rubbing his temple.

"Ugh," George said.

Halfway between the lodge and the Canteen, Seth Logan had taken Kylie's suitcase and was holding it up over his head. Jerry Magee had done the same with Kylie's sleeping bag. Kylie stood in between them crying.

"Come and get it diaper-wearer!" Seth said, sneering.

Abby made a beeline toward the two bullies. George followed her. She grabbed the sleeping bag from Jerry then turned to confront Seth.

"Get away from her, you knuckle-dragger!" she said as she kneeled to comfort Kylie.

George noticed Kylie crying and something switched inside him. It was as if someone had thrown a lever and given him a rush of adrenaline. He wasn't scared. He was mad.

"Give it back, Seth," George said, surprised by his own confidence.

"Well, well, if it isn't Georgie-poo."

"I said, give it back."

"What's it to you, Georgie?"

"She's my sister."

"Oh, is this your pink suitcase? I should have known."

Jerry laughed at the ruffian's joke.

"You'd better give it back or I'll— "

"Or you'll what?" Seth said, lowering the suitcase. He edged closer to George until he was right in his face. He had found a new victim. George held his ground. "What are you going to do, Georgie?"

John and Peter walked up and stood behind George.

"Leave us alone, Seth," John said. "We outnumber you."

"Yeah," Peter said. "You may get a few punches in, but you can't take on all of us at once."

Abby stood and took her place next to the boys. A small crowd had started to form.

"What's it going to be, losers? You gonna let everyone see you get beat up by a bunch of fifth-graders?"

Seth realized he had lost this round. "You guys are dead meat," he said. "Maybe not now, but just you wait. When you least expect it— BAM!—you're dead! Don't worry. If I don't get you first, the Howler will get ya soon enough!"

"Oh, George," Kylie said, crying harder now, "is the Howler gonna eat me?"

"Get lost creep!" Abby demanded.

Seth took Kylie's suitcase and tossed it into the tall weeds. "Argh!" he screamed in Kylie's face.

Kylie took off, running down the path. But instead of heading toward the Canteen, she missed the turn and ran straight into the woods.

10.

SETH HAD scared the daylights out of George's little sister Kylie. But it came as no surprise to George that Kylie would have gotten so scared when Seth started ranting about the Howler. Kylie had just finished first grade. The scary costumes on Halloween still gave her the creeps. George still didn't know what to make of the Howler either—and he was going into middle school.

As soon as Kylie ran off, Abby chased after her, and the two of them disappeared into the woods, following one of the many side trails that snaked off from the lodge.

George, John, and Peter followed them, but when they rounded the first bend in the trail, the two of them were nowhere to be seen.

"Kylie! Abby!" the three of them yelled, calling out in all directions.

"Where'd they go? They were right here?" George asked, concerned.

The three of them split up, heading briefly down the side trails looking for signs of them. Moments later, they returned to where they had separated.

"Where could they be?" George asked.

"They couldn't have gotten far," John replied.

"Wait a minute," Peter said. "What's that?"

"What's what?"

"Don't you hear that? I hear crying."

The three of them stopped and listened. A faint whimpering came from a short distance away.

"Come on!"

The three of them took off down the trail, skipping and dodging the random branchlets swatting at their legs. They stopped when they reached a fork in the path.

"Now where?" John said, panting.

"I don't know. Be quiet for a second." The three of them held their breath and strained their ears, trying to discern which way to go.

The crying had gotten louder.

"Something must be wrong," Peter said. "Now I hear Abby crying, too!"

"This way," Peter said, sprinting down the right fork in the path.

As they rounded the bend, they saw Abby leaning face-first against a tree with her head in her hands.

"Oh no!" George said.

They saw Kylie not far away huddling behind a bush.

"Seven, eight, nine, ten. Ready or not here I come!"

"That's not crying," John said. "It's laughing."

The three of them ran over to Abby.

"Oh, there you are," Abby said. "What kept ya?"

"What are you doing?" Peter asked.

"Kylie was upset, so I asked her if she wanted to play hide and seek. It's her favorite game."

Abby was right. It was Kylie's favorite game. It was smart thinking. Kylie didn't seem upset at all anymore. She giggled and laughed like nothing had ever happened.

"Thanks, Abby," George said. "Those guys are idiots."

Abby smiled.

"Hey guys," John said, "we had better head back. They've probably started already."

Abby looked around.

"She's over there," Peter said, pointing to Kylie hiding behind the bush.

Abby snuck up on Kylie. "Boo! I found you!" Kylie let out a joyful squeal. "Okay, Kylie," Abby said. "Time to go back and find your Kitty Cabin."

"Yea! Kitty Cabin!" Kylie cheered.

The three of them walked back toward the lodge, gathered their gear, and headed into the Canteen.

The Calamity Canteen served as the indoor meeting space at Camp Calamity. With heavy round logs for walls and a red metal roof, the Canteen looked like something off a syrup bottle, which, in George's mind, made it the perfect building for a cafeteria.

When they got inside, the campers were seated at long tables that stretched the length of the room. Knapsacks, suitcases, and sleeping bags cluttered the tabletops and the floor around them. Light streamed in from the large windows on the opposite side of the room, which overlooked Lake Mongoose, Camp Calamity's lake. About a dozen teenaged counselors stood around the campers, who sat quietly, listening to Mr. Jensen. One of the counselors corralled the five of them around a table in the back.

"That means," Mr. Jensen said, in the middle of his remarks, "there are going to be a few changes around here this week. First and foremost, you are to tell your counselor where you are and where you'll be at all times. Now, I know that a lot of you middle-schoolers like to head out fishing early in the mornings. That's fine; just let your counselors know where you'll be ahead of time. Second, there will be no unsupervised hikes in the woods, and the upper woods leading to the Hollow are off-limits. Last, but not least, and I realize this will be upsetting to some of you, but I'm counting on you to have a good attitude about this." Mr. Jensen paused, letting his warning sink in. After a moment, he continued. "The middle-schoolers will not be camping out in the lean-tos in the upper field this year."

"What? Oh no!" George said, unable to control his displeasure. He wasn't alone. Just about every middle-schooler in the room either moaned or let out an anguished cry. Some of them even wept. As the realization of what Mr. Jensen said settled in around the room, more campers either voiced their disappointment or dissolved into tearful wrecks right there in the Canteen. It seemed that mayhem day was living up to its name, as the camp counselors moved about the room trying to console those most aggrieved.

"This is awful," George said.

"It's more than awful—it sucks toads," Peter replied.

George glanced at his backpack. All those badges. All that work!

"Now calm down, calm down everyone," Mr. Jensen said, trying to be empathetic. "I know you're upset. Trust me. We didn't want to do it, but, as you older campers know, it's for your own safety. It's better to err on the side of caution than to be sorry later."

"Yeah, right," Peter muttered under his breath.

"Now, we want to try to make it up to you. So, we're giving the middle-schoolers—and only the middle-schoolers—an extra hour before lights out every night!" A collective *Yeah!* and *All right!* went up around the room. "And," Mr. Jensen continued, "we're going to let the middle-schoolers pick their own cabins and cabin-mates this year!"

Peter grabbed George and John, who were sitting next to him. His eyes were as big as saucers, and his mouth hung open. He didn't know what to say. None of them did. They just screamed and laughed as the rest of the middle-schoolers celebrated throughout the room.

"We're going to dismiss the elementary school campers first, and then, when they have left with their counselors, we will dismiss the middle-schoolers to find their bunks in Cabins 14 through 19."

"14 through 19?" George repeated, "Aren't they the older cabins on the ridge overlooking the lake?"

"Those things are dumps!" Peter said, "They haven't been used in years!"

"Look on the bright side," John said, "at least it's far away from the Kitty Cabins, and it's as close to the upper field as we can get. So," he whispered, "it'll be a perfect location to launch our secret mission."

II.

AFTER MAKING sure George's sister found her way to the second-grade counselor, the four friends joined the mad rush to claim a cabin. Most of the crowd headed for the ones closest to the lake. George and his friends, however, headed up the hill to the cabin nearest the woods. It was the farthest cabin from the lodge and the closest one to the trailhead that would take them to the upper field from where they planned to launch their secret mission. Seth and Jerry bullied their way into the first cabin by the lake, and George and his friends were glad that they would be as far away from them as possible.

After Abby claimed her bunk in one of the girls' cabins close by, the four friends stood outside of the last cabin: number 19.

"This place *is* a dump," John said, looking at the dilapidated structure. "Even the termites have abandoned this place."

"Why does it have hair?" Peter asked.

"That's not hair. That's moss."

"Same thing."

Since they had built the Kitty Cabins, Camp Calamity had made little use of the older cabins that sat atop the ridge overlooking Lake Mongoose, and the neglected structures had started to show their wear. The moss-covered roof of Cabin 19 slumped to the side, and the rickety shutters hung lopsided on their hinges. A large rip in the screen door flapped in the breeze.

"Well, I guess there's no use standing around. We'd better claim our bunks before the other kids get here," George said.

The wood creaked as the three boys trudged up the stairs and onto the porch.

"That'll never keep the mosquitos out," John said, inspecting the rip in the screen. "We'll be eaten alive!"

"At least it will be almost like we're sleeping outside," Peter replied.

"Don't worry," George said, "I'll fix it." He rummaged through his backpack and found his duct tape.

While the outside of the cabin had fallen into disrepair, the inside was remarkably clean. It looked like someone had spent some time hurrying to try to fix it up. The cabin consisted of three rooms: two large bunk rooms on the wings, one to the right, the other to the left, and a small counselor's room in the middle. A brand-new whiteboard hung on the wall to the left of the door. Abby and Peter peeked into the counselor's room, which stood empty at the moment. A stack of folded clothes lay on the bed.

"Hey, come over here and look at this," George said, still inspecting the tear in the screen.

"What is it?" Abby asked as the four of them crowded around.

George held the pieces of the screen together. "Look to the sides of the tear. Do you see the creases?"

"Yeah," I see 'em," John said, "so what?"

"Don't you think it looks like a claw mark?"

"Yeah, you know what," Peter said. "It does."

"Hold on," George said, rummaging through his backpack again. He removed the disposable camera Peter had given him and took a picture.

Abby held up her hand in front of the four long gashes. The two outside ones made the rough shape of a 'Y,' while the two inner ones ran parallel to each other. "That would have to be a huge claw," she said, wondering aloud. She inspected the screen, methodically moving her head back and forth. "Wait a minute," she said, "I'll be right back." She ran to her cabin and came back with a pair of tweezers, a baggie, and a black marker. "Hold the screen up again," she said. She leaned in to get a closer look. Then she maneuvered the tweezers between her fingers and yanked something out of the mesh.

"What is it?" Peter asked.

"I have no clue," Abby said.

"It looks like a black thorn or something," George said.

"It could be the tip of a claw," John replied. Abby dropped the mysterious clue into the baggie and labeled it with the black marker as several boys rushed down the path toward their cabin.

George put away the camera and ripped off a long strip of duct tape. He repaired the slice in the screen, creating a long, perfect seam, after which he joined his friends inside.

George, John, and Peter each claimed a bunk in the room to the right, as the four boys rushed through the front door. Abby casually positioned herself in the doorway to her friends' room, so none of the other boys could sneak in and grab the extra bunk. Shocked by seeing a girl in the boys' cabin, the four boys kept their distance and claimed four other bunks in the room to the left.

"I'm gonna go back to my cabin and unpack," Abby said when she was sure her friends had staked out their territory. "Catch you later?"

"Sure," George replied.

Before long, the four friends had unpacked their gear and had their sleeping bags spread out across their bunks. They spent the rest of the day swimming, hiking, fishing, and checking out the new obstacle course on the other side of camp. When they returned to their cabin before dinner, they found a lanky, red-haired teen sitting on the bunk in the counselor's room.

"Hey, guys," he said cheerfully. "I'm Jack." "Everyone having fun?"

"Yeah, loads," Peter replied, as the others nodded in agreement.

"Would you all mind writing your names on the whiteboard outside my door?" Jack said. "That way, I can keep track of you. I'll be roaming around camp checking in on you from time to time. But if you can't find me, just make sure you write on the board where you're headin', so I know where you are."

After dinner around dusk, the middle-schoolers met at the fire pit down by the lake. The pit was surrounded on three sides by several rows of wooden logs that had been hewn into benches. George, John, Peter, and Abby found a space in the front row to the right. The six middle school counselors, one from each cabin, stood between the fire and the lake. Counselor Jack noticed George and his friends and gave them a wave and a nod.

George had been quite bummed they wouldn't get a chance to cook their dinners over an open campfire in front of the lean-tos, but he was happy when Counselor Jack pulled out some hotdogs and marshmallows. He handed some skewers to George and his friends and told them they could each roast a hotdog and make a s'more.

Daylight seeped from the day in a reddish glow, and the camp counselors took turns leading the kids singing silly songs. George and his friends were thrilled that their counselor knew the craziest ones. George especially liked the one about sticking french fries up your nose and putting dill pickles between your toes.

As darkness settled in, the counselors passed around popcorn and told ghost stories. The stories weren't scary to George, just a little spooky. Of course, his sister Kylie would have been horrified if she were there. As they started the third story, Mr. Jensen interrupted them and pulled the counselors away from the group. When they were out of earshot, Seth and Jerry made their move.

"All you puny fifth-graders better be on guard tonight," Seth said.

"Yeah," Jerry taunted, "you'd better learn how to sleep with one eye open, or the Howler might drag you off into the woods."

"The Howler?" one of the campers, clearly a newbie, asked.

"The Horrible Hollow Howler," Seth said, in the most menacing voice that he could muster.

"What's that?"

"Some say the Howler's a prehistoric beast that lurks in these woods. They say it was accidentally awoken from its thousand-year hibernation by some unsuspecting camper who wandered into its lair around the time this camp opened."

"Some say it's a werewolf," Jerry added.

"Others say it was once a man," Seth said, "possibly the old Camp Calamity caretaker from the 1920s, who got lost in the woods and went crazy when he couldn't find his way out of the Hollow. They say he was transformed into a beast when he was forced to eat the living flesh of wild animals—and later the campers themselves."

"Yeah," Jerry added, "whatever the Howler is, it comes back every so often to feed. On moonlit nights it roams the woods, looking for its next victim."

"And now it's come back. The counselors have heard it howling out in the deep woods for weeks."

"They've even heard it crunching on bones!"

"The last time it returned, a young camper got separated from his hiking group and was never heard from again."

"Some say it has bad eyesight, so it can't tell the difference between an animal and a person. They say if you ever run into it if you stand really still and don't make a sound it won't get you! That's why the woods get really quiet whenever it's around. The animals have learned how to avoid it."

"That's just a baby story," one of the braver campers said, daring to contradict Seth and his sidekick. "They just tell that story to scare the little kids in the Kitty Cabins."

"Oh yeah?" Seth said. "Tell that to the Nussbaum's cat, or the Albertson's dog, or the Davison's chickens—not to mention their goat!"

"What happened to their goat?" someone asked.

"Didn't ya hear? It was ripped to shreds!"

"Yeah, a hundred and fifty-pound deer was, too! Seth and I overheard Sheriff Brown tellin' Mr. Walter about it at the hardware store. Don't believe us? Just ask those losers over there," Jerry said, pointing at George and his friends. "They were there. They heard it, too."

Abby stood. "We didn't hear nothin' you imbeciles!"

"The Howler's not real," the brave camper said. "You're just trying to scare us."

Just then, a terrifying sound echoed through the woods. It sounded so bizarre and out of place, it made George's blood run cold. Something had screamed. At first, he thought it was an animal, but then he wasn't sure. It almost sounded like his little sister's shrieks when she wakes in the middle of the night from a nightmare. Except this scream sounded inhuman. Then it echoed again, this time louder and much closer. Several campers gasped. George looked at the faces of the kids sitting closest to the fire, but the only thing he saw was the red glow of fear.

12.

GEORGE AND his friends sat around the campfire in front of the lake with their backs to the woods. Moments before, they had been enjoying themselves, singing songs, roasting marshmallows, and eating hotdogs with the counselors and other campers. Then they had heard something horrifying. Something had screamed in the woods. Something that sounded not quite like an animal yet not altogether human. The red-orange glow of the fire reflected off the faces of the frightened campers and forged long shadows that ran deep into the blackness of the night. Whatever the source of the screaming, it seemed to be getting closer, creeping towards them from the concealing shelter of the darkness. Soon it would reveal its horrible presence in the small circle of light of the campfire.

With unimaginable certainty, the creature stepped from the woods, and George and his friends widened their eyes, trying to defy the dark to discern a monstrous shape. But something confounded their senses. The creature's voice seemed to grow smaller, now that it had freed itself from the echoes of the woods. Still in the shadows, the wailing creature edged toward the firelight, and George and his friends found themselves casting their eyes toward the ground at something small, rather than the large creature they had envisioned emerging from the woods.

The small beast stepped into the ring of light, and George and his friends tried to reconcile the reality of what they saw with the runaway visions of their imaginations.

"It's Mrs. Nussbaum's cat!" someone yelled. "It's Jeepers!"

It was.

The cat staggered and swayed with its head listing to one side. It seemed to be drawn to the firelight. Its eyes darted back and forth, swinging from side to side like a pendulum. Although they looked odd, they were not at all menacing. The hair on the cat's back lay dirty and matted, its feet and claws stained with black dirt. It looked as though it had spent most of its time recently burrowing in the mud. The cat slumped to the ground next to the fire, exhausted.

Responding to the commotion, the counselors rushed back to the campfire. One of them bent down and stroked the haggard cat. It shuddered slightly when the counselor placed her hand on its coat. The cat looked up at her with soft eyes. It was the same gentle expression that had endeared Jeepers to George and his classmates in the first place. It was then they realized that the cat meant them no harm, but had sought out their help after experiencing some unknown and traumatic experience.

"What's the matter with her?" Peter asked as everyone crowded around Jeepers.

"It's hard to say," John said, "but it looks quite scared."

"It looks like it got into some catnip," Peter said.

"Why do you think it's so dirty?" George asked.

The counselor lifted the cat onto her lap. Some of its hair was missing. It had two long and thin bare marks down the center of its back, and two similar marks on each of its sides. To George and his friends, the scratches looked eerily familiar.

"It looks to me like it's been hiding," Abby said. "You know, digging holes under logs and stuff?"

"Hiding from what?" Peter asked though he didn't have to. The others had been asking themselves that same question. The four of them looked out at the dark woods.

"Whatever it was," Abby said, "it scared Jeepers enough to keep her from going home."

"Alright, let's break it up," Mr. Jensen said, pushing through the crowd of kids. "That's enough excitement for one night. Seth and Jerry," he said, turning to the two eighth-graders, "are these yours?" Mr. Jensen held out two rubber werewolf masks.

"I've never seen them before in my life!" Seth said, clearly lying.

"Then why did we find them hidden under your mattresses?"

"Someone must have planted them!"

"A first-grade counselor saw you two wearing them and scaring little kids down at the Kitty Cabins."

"That's a lie!" Jerry said.

"I'm afraid you two will have to spend the night in the lodge, so go get your things."

"But—"

"One more word and you'll sleep there for the rest of the week." Seth and Jerry slunk back to their cabin to get their gear, much to the satisfaction of the other campers. "As for the rest of you," Mr. Jensen said, "it's time to call it a night."

"What's going to happen to Jeepers?" Someone asked.

"We'll keep her down at the lodge for tonight. I'll drive her back to Mrs. Nussbaum's tomorrow. I'm sure she'll be happy to see her."

George and his friends said goodnight to Abby as they passed by her cabin, and the three boys twisted their way up the trail to Cabin 19, complaining all the way about the hasty end to their evening. Inside the cabin, the faint yellow glow from a single electric lightbulb in each room illuminated the space, and the three boys climbed the ladder to George's top bunk.

"Lights out in forty-five minutes, okay guys?" Jack said, peeking his head in the door.

"What do you think happened to Jeepers?" Peter asked.

"I agree with Abby," John said. "I think she was hiding from something."

"If you ask me, I'd bet it was the Howler," Peter said, "or whatever that thing is out there killing those animals."

"She could have just gotten lost," George suggested.

"Not likely," John said, "did you notice the scratches on her back? They formed the same pattern as the ones on the screen door. Four gashes: the two outside ones in the shape of a 'Y' and two parallel ones in the middle."

"That's probably why she was hiding," Peter said. "Something was chasing her."

"Jeepers is the fastest cat I've ever seen," George said, "probably faster than a rabbit. It's definitely faster than a goat."

"Well, whatever she was running from," John said, "judging by the scratches on her back, it looks as though she barely escaped with her life."

"I'd say she probably lost at least one of her nine lives," Peter said.

Before lights out, the three of them decided they would get up early the next day and head down to the lodge to take pictures of Jeepers' injuries before Mr. Jensen took her back to Mrs. Nussbaum. They'd also have Abby inspect the scratches on her back in more detail.

Soon after Jack turned off the light, John and Peter settled into deep rhythmic breathing and drifted off to sleep, and George lay there listening to the buzzing katydids and chirping crickets. It wasn't long before Peter's snoring was added to the mix. It had been a long and eventful first day, and soon George's eyes, too, grew heavy with sleep.

Lingering in the twilight between wakefulness and dreams, the moment after he had drifted off to sleep, George was startled awake, not by a sound, but by the absence of sound. Something had caused the crickets, katydids, and other night creatures to halt their buzzes and chirps. George lay there for some time, staring at the blue light filtering through the cabin's murky windows, wondering what might be lurking in the night. More than once he could have sworn he saw a dark shadow move across the window. It wasn't until the wee hours past midnight, when the crickets and katydids returned, that George was finally able to drift off to sleep.

13.

GEORGE SAT at the breakfast table in the Calamity Canteen with his head propped up on his hands. Today was one day he was glad he didn't have to cook his own breakfast. He sat with his eyes half open and his cheeks full of syrup-mushy pancakes. Abby emerged from the breakfast line, and George moved his yellow disposable camera so she could sit next to him.

"Hey, guys! How'd you sleep?" Abby asked, sounding cheerful, a little too cheerful for George.

"Great!" John replied. "It's so peaceful here."

George moaned.

"I slept like a rock," Peter said, happily gnawing on some bacon, oblivious to George's sleepiness.

"I know you did," George said. "You snored all night."

"I know. I know. I'm sorry," Peter said, sounding remorseful. "My mom says I always snore when I'm really tired."

"What's wrong, George?" Abby said. "You seem a little irritated."

"I was up half the night," George replied.

"I'm sorry, George," Peter said. "I'll try not to snore tonight."

"No, Peter, it's not that. It wasn't you. It's just . . ." He wondered if he should go on. "Last night, outside the cabin, I could have sworn I saw . . . oh, never mind," he said, changing his mind. He didn't want to admit that he had been spooked.

The three friends stopped eating and looked at him.

"Could have sworn you saw what, George?" John asked.

George looked around to make sure no one else was listening. "Do you guys remember last night around the campfire, when Seth and Jerry were saying something about how the animals get really quiet whenever the Howler's around."

"Yeah, I remember that," Peter said. "I've heard that before. Rumor has it that the Howler has bad eyesight, so it uses its sensitive hearing to find its prey. Whenever the Howler's around, the animals stand really still and get super quiet, so the Howler won't find them."

"Yeah, that's right," John said. "I also heard that the bright light hurts its eyes."

"Well, last night, just as I was drifting off to sleep, the woods got really quiet. I was laying there listening to the crickets and katydids when all of a sudden . . . nothing."

"And . . ." John said, egging George on. He could tell there was more that George wasn't telling them.

"And . . . I could have sworn I saw something pass by the window."

The three friends looked at each other.

"What!"

"No way!"

"Why didn't you wake us?"

"Yeah, it was probably the Howler!"

"I don't know. I don't know," George said. "I wasn't sure what it was. I thought it was probably the counselors or something. Then I remembered this morning that the same thing happened a few nights ago when I was taking Buster for a walk."

Peter's fork dropped from his hand and clinked on his plate. "You're kidding!"

"Really?"

"What happened?"

"Why didn't you tell us?"

"Buster was acting really strange, growling and barking at the woods. Then he yanked the leash and got away from me. My neighbor,

Mr. Furgeson, caught him. He just so happened to be coming back from his nightly run."

"Did he see anything?"

"I asked him, and he said he didn't."

"Not a thing?"

"Nope, but something sure spooked Buster."

"It could have been a squirrel or a deer or something," Abby said.

"That's what I thought at first," George said, "but then something strange happened. Just before Buster and I reached the sidewalk, I could have sworn a dark figure crossed the jogging path near the edge of the woods, just like the shadow passed by the window last night."

"It could have been your imagination playing tricks on you," John added.

"Maybe," George said. "I'm just not sure."

"We should investigate outside the cabin after we check on Jeepers," John said.

"That's what I was thinking," Peter agreed.

The four of them stopped by the lodge after breakfast to check on Jeepers. Mr. Jensen said that it was kind of them to stop by. Each of them took turns stroking her soft coat, making sure they rubbed the fur behind her ears. Jeepers always liked it when they did that.

Although it was obvious that she had been through a tough time, Jeepers seemed happy to see them and purred when Abby held her on her lap. Peter took pictures of the scratch marks on Jeepers' back, and Abby inspected them up close. The four friends were positive that they were an exact match of the rip on the screen door to Cabin 19.

They said goodbye to Jeepers and Mr. Jensen and headed down the winding path toward Lake Mongoose. Although it was still early, the camp buzzed with activity. Several boats dotted the lake, and a half dozen fishermen lined the shore. The four friends stopped by Abby's cabin so she could pick up her backpack and headed up the trail toward Cabin 19.

"Which window were you looking through when you noticed the shadow?" John asked when they reached the cabin.

"The one in the far corner," George replied.

"Let's spread out and see what we can find."

Abby searched along the side of the cabin, while John and Peter scoured the weeds along the tree line. George zigzagged in between them, moving back and forth across the grass between the cabin and the woods.

"George," Abby called from the corner of the cabin, "come over here and look at this." George made his way over to Abby. "What is it?"

"Do you see how this grass is matted down right here?" She said, pointing along the cabin's foundation. "Do you see how the stems are all broken and laying over on themselves?"

"Yeah? So what?"

"Move your hand along the ground where the grass is broken." George did. "Do you feel the indentation in the ground and how it's kind of sunk in a little where the grass is bent?"

"Yeah, I do."

"Something heavy walked through here—really heavy." She stood and looked over the ground again. "Which way did you see the shadow moving last night?"

"It started over that way," George said, pointing toward the woods. "Then it made its way down here, passed the window at the back of the cabin, rounded the corner, and passed the window on the side."

"You say it came from this direction?" Abby said, walking toward the woods.

"Yeah."

She stopped at a bare patch of ground and knelt.

"Guys, everyone, come here quick!" she said.

The three boys ran to Abby. She lifted a long tuft of grass off a patch of dirt revealing a paw print—a rather large paw print.

"Holy Moly!" Peter said. "I knew it! It's the Howler."

"Whatever it is, it's huge," John said.

"George, take a picture," Abby said, spreading the grass out away from the print. George removed the disposable camera and took several shots.

"It kind of looks like a dog footprint," George said.

"It's too big to be a dog," John said. "Maybe it's a bear."

"Hold on!" Peter said, running to the cabin. He returned with his backpack. He sat it on the ground and started rummaging through it. "I took this from my dad's hunting gear," he said, removing a book with hard plastic pages.

"What's that?" George asked.

"It's a field guide for tracking animals." Peter flipped through the pages until he found what he sought. "There," he said, pointing at the page. "That's a bear print."

"It doesn't look the same," Abby said. "Bears have five toes, and they all point toward the front of the foot. The tracks only have four toes."

Peter flipped through the stiff pages again. He stopped at a page that depicted several sets of footprints, all of them looked remarkably similar. "Look at the shape," Peter said. "All of these prints are from animals that have slightly rounded, triangle-shaped pads on their paw with four toes: two on the outside forming the shape of a 'Y,' and two in the middle toward the front of the foot."

"It's the same pattern as the scratch on Jeepers' back and the screen door."

"Let's make a deduction," John said. "Jeepers came out of the woods pretty close to the cabin, the claw marks on the screen door match the ones on Jeepers' back, and the paw prints match both Jeepers and the claw marks on the door. What can we infer from this?"

"They all came from the same animal," George said.

"Correct," John replied.

"I'm so glad you didn't say they were picking boogers," Abby said.

"But look," Peter said, pointing to the page. "Do you see these prints? All of them are from the canine family. The smallest one is a fox. The next two are a dog and a coyote. Do you see the largest one?"

"Yeah."

"That's a wolf."

"So you're saying that this is a wolf track," Abby said.

"No, that's not what I'm saying. Look at the sizes. The wolf print is about five inches wide. This track has to be at least double that."

"So this track was made by something bigger than a wolf?"

"That's exactly what I'm saying. The wolf or animal that made this track," Peter said, pointing to the paw print in the book, "was probably about thirty inches tall."

"So, if the animal that made this print is double that size . . ."

"It has to be about sixty inches tall."

"Sixty inches tall," George said. "That's—"

"Five feet," John said, cutting him off. "We're talking about a wolf or some kind of canine that's five feet tall."

"Five feet!"

"And that's walking on four legs. Think how tall it would be if it walked on two."

"Abby's the tallest one here," George said, "and she's only four feet tall."

The four of them gazed at the woods, trying to imagine a five-foot-tall wolf coming out of the tree line. George looked down at the paw print then back toward the cabin. In his mind, he retraced the path that the creature took, following its imaginary steps down from the woods, to the paw print where the four of them stood, and finally to the cabin. He drew an imaginary arrow on the ground from the cabin to the paw print until he had a pretty good idea where the creature must have come out of the woods.

"Did you guys check over that way for clues?" George asked, pointing in the direction he had traced in his mind's eye.

"Yeah, we searched all over there in the weeds. We didn't find anything."

"You only searched the weeds?"

"Yeah."

"I think we need to look a little higher," he said.

George walked up the hill, heading for a patch of low hanging branches near where he thought the beast had come out of the thicket of trees. George's friends followed. They walked along the tree line as George inspected the branches that hung out of reach. Finally, he found a broken branch. He entered the woods and found another one. The friends followed the trail of broken branches until George spotted what he had been seeking.

14.

GEORGE PULLED down the tree branch that held the broken twig. "There," he said.

"Holy Cow!" John said. "It's our first piece of hard evidence."

Hanging from the end of the broken twig was a long tuft of coarse gray hair that looked almost black.

"Don't touch it," Abby said. "George, take a picture."

George snapped a few pictures with his disposable camera while Abby removed a specimen jar and tweezers from her backpack.

"Peter, pull down the branch again," she said.

Abby reached up and dislodged the tuft of hair from the branch with the tweezers. She deposited it into the specimen jar.

"That's why it looks like a shadow," Peter said as Abby held the jar up to the sunlight. "It's almost black."

Abby labeled the jar with a black marker and stowed everything in her backpack. They looked at the trail of broken branches up ahead. It stretched as far as they could see into the deep woods.

"How far do you think it goes?" Peter asked.

"I don't know," George replied.

"Looks like it's heading in the direction of the upper field," Abby said.

"That would make sense," John replied, "if it came from the Hollow."

"Hey, you kids need to get out of there!" someone yelled from outside the tree line. "The woods are off-limits." It was Counselor Jack.

The four friends trudged back toward the cabin. Their feet crunched on a thin layer of dry leaves.

"We're heading to the archery course for some target practice," Counselor Jack said when they stepped from the tree line. "Why don't you all come along? It'll keep you out of trouble."

They reluctantly agreed.

Peter, John, and Abby followed Counselor Jack back to the cabin. George, however, lingered at the edge of the woods, near where he had spotted the first broken tree branch. He walked over to the branch and snapped a picture. They had all assumed that the creature walked on all fours, like a wolf, but what if it didn't? He thought for a moment and looked up. Over his head, about ten feet in the air, was another broken twig. A long tuft of black hair hung from the end of it.

15.

"THAT'S IMPOSSIBLE," Abby said, threading another arrow onto her bow. "A ten-foot-tall wolf?" She drew back on the bow-string and let the arrow fly. It hit the outer edge of the bullseye.

"Good shot," Peter said.

"Thanks."

"I'm just telling you what I saw," George replied, taking his turn at the target.

"I still say it's impossible."

George's arrow pierced one of the outer rings. He frowned.

"Keep both eyes open when you aim."

"Okay."

"It's not impossible," Peter said, fumbling with his bow. "If a five-foot-tall wolf walked on its hind legs, it could be about ten feet tall if it's standing upright."

"Well, it's not likely," Abby said.

Peter shrugged and took his shot. It missed the target completely and hit a tree.

"Nuts!"

"I agree with Peter," John said, stepping up for his turn. "We're inferring from the tracks that Abby found and the claw marks on the screen that the creature we're looking for is a wolf."

"Which would make sense since they call it the Howler," Peter added.

"Don't forget the scratches on Jeepers' back," George said. "They match a wolf's claw marks perfectly."

"Right," John said, "but what if it's not a wolf. What if it's something like a wolf, but it's not a wolf?"

"You mean like a gorilla is similar to a monkey, but it's not a monkey," Abby said.

"Right," John said, pulling back on the bowstring until it touched his nose. "Remember, it could be a cryptid or some other Bigfoot-like creature that hasn't been discovered yet. Scientists have known about squids for a long time. But up until a hundred years ago, they thought that giant squids were a myth. They never even captured one on film until ten years ago." John let go of the arrow. It sailed toward the target and stuck between George and Abby's arrows. "We need to keep an open mind about this before we draw the wrong conclusion."

The four friends walked to the next target on the course.

"Abby, you're up."

Abby threaded her bow again and pulled back on the string. Her shot landed dead center of the bullseye.

"Nice shot!" Peter said.

"You always beat me!" George replied.

Abby grinned.

"I think we need to put the first part of our plan into action tonight," John said.

"Are you still sure about this?" George asked. "That thing has to be huge."

"It's what we planned for," Peter replied. "That's why we brought our weapons."

"We've got a hatchet, a slingshot, a pocket knife, and pepper spray."

"Don't forget Abby."

"Right we've got Abby, too. But, do you really think a little pocket knife or a slingshot can protect us from a ten-foot-tall wolf?"

"We don't have to get close to it," John said. "We just have to get a picture. We'll find a good spot and set up Peter's game camera. Then we can go back later to see if it captured anything."

"Come on, George," Peter said. "Don't bail on us now. We need you."

"What do you think, Abby?"

"I think the odds are still good that it's not the Howler, so I think we'll be safe."

"What about the tuft of hair up in that tree?"

"It could have come from a squirrel or something. Either way, I still say we need to get to the bottom of it."

"What'd you say, George? We can sneak out tonight after lights out and hike up to the upper lean-tos," John said. "That'll be a perfect place to stake out the Howler as it comes up from Calamity Hollow."

"So," someone sneered from behind them, "you turds are going after the Howler." The four friends turned as Seth and Jerry stepped out of the woods behind them. "That has got to be the stupidest thing I've ever heard," Seth said, pushing through the shrubs.

"Spying on us again, Seth?" Abby said.

"I don't know what you're talking about."

"You know what she means," George said. "You guys were spying on us that day in Walter's Hardware Store, the day we heard Mr. Walter and Sheriff Brown talking about the Howler."

"I knew you turds were up to something, but you won't go through with it. You're too scared. Remember what happened to that deer—and the Davison's goat?" Seth made a ripping sound with his teeth. "Torn to bits."

"Why don't you just shut-up, Seth!" Abby said.

"You think you're pretty big standing there with that bow in your hand."

"I don't need this bow, and you know it!"

"You'll need more than that if the Howler comes. It'll tear you apart!"

"That's for sure," Jerry said. "The last time the Howler came back, a young camper got separated from his hiking group and was never heard from again!"

"Well, that's not exactly true," Seth added. "The counselors did try to find him for three days. Each night they heard him shrieking in the woods as the Howler slowly ripped off chunks of his flesh and ate him alive. All they ever found was his shredded clothes and a few gnawed-on bones! Some say at night you can still hear his ghost screaming."

"You're just trying to scare us, Seth!" Abby said.

"Oh, I'll bet you're scared all right. As a matter of fact, I'll bet you won't even go to the lean-tos tonight! You'll chicken out."

"Oh, we're going, Seth," George said. "Unless you're going to tell on us or something."

"Trust me. I won't tell. I actually can't wait to see you try!"

"Okay, I'll take you up on that bet, Seth."

Seth looked shocked. "What do you mean?" he said.

"You said you bet we're all too scared to go to the lean-tos and that you can't wait to see us try," George said. "The only way you'll be able to see us is if you spend the night up there yourselves."

"George, what are you doing?" John said, pulling him aside.

"Trust me." George stepped closer to Seth and Jerry. "I'll bet we *will* spend all night in the lean-tos and that we can make it longer than you!"

A grin appeared across Seth's face. "Oh, this is going to be fun, Georgie. One of two things is going to happen. Either you're going to get scared and go running back to the cabins, or you and your friends are going to get ripped apart by the Howler. Either way, it's going to be hilarious!"

"We'll meet you in the Upper fields at lights out—unless you're too scared," George said.

"You're on, Georgie!"

Seth and Jerry turned to leave.

"One last thing, Seth."

"What's that, Georgie?"

"If we win, you and Jerry will leave us alone, and you'll never bully my friends or me again!"

Seth looked at Jerry and sneered.

"And if *we* win, you're dead."

16.

AT LIGHTS out, George, John, and Peter crawled out the back window and made their way to the trailhead leading to the upper field. They had arranged to meet Abby at the trailhead. Before they left, John had tiptoed to the whiteboard outside Counselor Jack's room and scrawled "gone fishing" beside each of their names. They hoped it would buy them some time if Counselor Jack woke early and wondered where they were.

The three friends snuck past the remaining cabins in silence, a strange blue light from a full moon illuminated their way. When they rounded the corner, Abby was waiting for them at the trailhead.

"Did you have any trouble?" Abby whispered when they arrived.

George shook his head. "Peter got his backpack caught on the screen, but other than that it was no problem."

"Has anyone seen Seth or Jerry?"

"No," George replied, "not yet."

"I still can't believe you dared those guys to come along," Peter said, trying to keep his voice low.

"Those two morons have bullied us for too long," George said. "This will settle it once and for all. Besides, I just didn't trust them not to tell on us. Now that they're coming along, they'll have to keep it a secret."

"Well, this is it," Abby said, turning toward the woods. "Is everyone ready?"

The four friends stared at the trail, cutting a steep path up the hill through the trees. Moonlight lit the winding path until it disappeared around the bend but no further. Long shadows stretched into the dark woods, sucking the light from the night like a black hole. George listened to the night sounds, and although they reassured him, he found them somewhat troubling. He couldn't help but wonder if they were a warning to turn back

"Peter, did you bring the game camera?" John asked.

Peter patted his backpack. "Check."

"How about you, George? Did you bring the map?"

"Yep, it's right here," he said, tapping the side pocket of his bag. "Does everyone have their weapons?" Everyone nodded. "Okay. I think we'd better have them ready from here on out."

The four friends moved to the edge of the woods with their weapons drawn then hesitated. They had reached the point of no return, and no one wanted to step onto the trail. George stood listening to the crickets and katydids, studying the rhythm and cadence of their calls. He looked up the trail and into the darkness and then at his friends, who stood there listening along with him.

"Okay," he said. "Let's go."

They cinched their packs close to their backs and stepped onto the trail. George took the lead.

17.

GEORGE AND his friends ascended the trail with slow and careful steps, carrying their weapons at their sides. George held his new hatchet, John his pocketknife, Peter his slingshot, and Abby her pepper spray. They ascended the trail in silence, taking note of the chorus of night sounds accompanying them. Although it lay only a short distance away, the terrain and lack of light made it a somewhat difficult climb. The upper field sat on top of a ridge about a half a mile from Camp Calamity's main cabins in a clearing about the size of a football field.

The four friends approached the entrance to the field, which sat awash in the blue light from the moon. They scanned the dark triangles of lean-tos lining the northern and eastern edges. There was no sign of Seth or Jerry.

"I guess they chickened out," Peter said.

"Don't count on it," Abby replied. "If I had to guess, I'd say they were around here somewhere."

"What's the plan?" George asked.

"First, we need to find a safe place to hide and watch," John said. "Then we need to find a good spot to set up the game camera."

"So you mean we're kind of like on a stakeout?" Peter asked.

"Yeah, that's right," John replied. "George, take out the map." George removed the map from the side pocket of his backpack. "Which direction is the Hollow?"

"Hold on," George said, removing a compass from his backpack. He oriented the map and positioned himself to face north. "It's that way, west," he said, pointing across the field.

"Okay," John said, "that's where the Howler will be coming up out of the Hollow."

"Right," Peter said.

"It will be flooded in moonlight as soon as it steps into the field, so we need to find a lean-to with our backs to the east."

"Why the east?" Peter asked.

"That's the direction that the moon rises," John said, "so we'll be in the shadows. If what they say about the Howler's eyesight is true, it will be blinded by the moonlight, so it won't be able to see us."

"Plus, our backs will be towards the camp," Abby added, "so it won't sneak up on us, either."

"Right."

The four friends searched for a lean-to that satisfied John's requirements and found one along the eastern side of the field. They threw their backpacks onto the elevated wooden platform comprising the lean-to's floor. Then they unrolled their sleeping bags and took stock of their gear. They would carry their packs and weapons with them always, just in case they needed to make a run for it.

"The first thing we need to do is set up the game camera across the field," John said. "It will be the most dangerous part of the mission. We don't want to give ourselves away, so we'll have to be quiet. But we don't want to sneak up on the Howler either."

"Yeah, if we accidentally surprise that thing we're dead meat," Peter said.

"We'll just have to be careful," John replied. "Peter, get the game camera ready. You'll need to set it up as quickly as you can. George, Abby, and I will stand guard."

"Right."

When Peter had the game camera ready, the four friends grabbed their backpacks and weapons and set off toward the western edge of the field. They crept along the tree line, letting the shadows hide their movements from the light of the moon.

Peter jumped onto the platform of the last lean-to. "Look," he whispered. "Seth and Jerry's backpacks are in here."

"I knew it," Abby said. "I knew they were around here somewhere."

"But where are they?" Peter asked.

George shined his flashlight around the upper field. "I don't know," he said. "But now we have more than one reason to be on our guard."

Peter jumped down from the platform, and the four friends tiptoed along the tree line. When they reached the western side of the field, George, John, and Abby fanned out around Peter and searched for a place to set up the game camera. John took the lead while George and Abby flanked Peter, one on each side.

George snapped his fingers, trying to get his friends' attention. They stopped, and he pointed to several broken branches on the edge of a thicket of trees. It revealed a well-worn path out of the darkness of the Hollow. John nodded, and the three friends entered the tree line. They made their way down the path until they found a slight clearing next to a large tree.

Peter went to work. He positioned the camera as high on the tree as he could. Then he threw the straps around the trunk and fastened them with Velcro. When he was sure it was secure, he toggled the power switch to the on position and pressed the button that configured the camera to its night vision setting.

"Okay," Peter whispered, "That should . . ."

From that moment on, the night was filled with screaming.

18.

THE SCREAMS echoed through the woods in a kind of shrieking that overwhelmed George's senses. At first, he stood frozen, too terrified to step from the spot where he stood. Then his instincts kicked in. He whirled to the right and then the left, squinting into the darkness to try to find the source of the terror that gripped him.

As far as he could tell, he was unhurt, but the fate of his friends eluded him. With each twist and turn, he expected to find one of them in the clutches of some unimaginable beast or lying on the ground in a pool of stomach-churning blood and gore. He saw Peter cowering behind a shrub, his face twisted in fear. John was covering his ears in a desperate attempt to block out the horrifying sounds. Abby ran toward him and grabbed Peter and John as she ran past.

"Come on!"

The four friends ran back to the tree line and bolted into the upper field. They stood in the moonlight, peering in the direction of the screams, piercing the quiet of the woods.

"What is that?" Abby yelled as the shrieking continued.

"I don't know!" George replied, still reeling from the sudden fracture of silence. "It sounds like people screaming!"

Somewhere in the woods, an intense rustling and crunching sound disturbed the undergrowth, and soon the shouts and shrieks turned to desperate pleas.

"Help! Please help! It's got us!" a voice cried from the dark.

"That's Seth!" John said.

"Help us! Someone, please help us!" another voice called.

"And that sure sounded a lot like Jerry," Peter said.

"Wait a minute," Abby said, as the screaming resumed. "They're just trying to scare us."

"How can you tell," George asked, still trying to make sense of it all.

"I don't know," she said. "I'm not sure."

"Maybe they really need our help," Peter said.

Somewhere in the distance, a deep and resonant growl grew into a howl, and the rustling and screaming stopped.

"Oh, no," George said. "What was that?"

"It, it . . . it sounded like an . . . an animal," John said.

"Why does it sound all echoey?" Abby asked, a little confused.

"Help us! Please help us!" the pleading resumed, this time from deeper in the woods.

"That definitely sounds like Seth," Abby said.

"That thing must be chasing them!" Peter added.

"I don't think so," Abby said. "I think they're trying to scare us."

"What do we do?" John asked.

"We could go back and get help," Peter said.

"That's what they want us to do," George replied. "They want us to get scared and go back, so we'll lose the bet."

"Plus we'll get in big trouble for being out of our bunks," John added.

"George, John, Peter, Abby! Help us!"

"Now they're calling for us," Peter said.

"But how did they know we were here?" Abby asked. "Unless they've been spying on us again."

"I think Abby's right," George said. "I'll bet they're just trying to scare us."

"But what if we're wrong?" Peter asked. "What if something really is chasing them?"

George was unsure of how to answer, and the longer he stood there, the more the weight of the question sunk in. Peter was right. They had no choice.

"We can't take that chance," George said. "If that thing is out there, then Seth and Jerry need our help. Does everyone still have their weapons?" They all nodded. "Okay, we'll have to be ready. Even if Seth and Jerry are trying to scare us, that thing is still out there." Everyone nodded. "Okay then, weapons and flashlights out. Let's go."

The four friends followed the screams, chasing after Seth and Jerry. The long white beams from their flashlights ricocheted in the darkness. The narrow path they followed twisted through the woods but in no clear direction. It snaked back and forth over itself in zigzags, confusing the friends as to the direction of the bullies. At one moment, it sounded as if they were in front of them, the next moment, behind them. After several twists and turns, the trail branched off in two directions, and the four friends stopped at the fork.

"Now where?" John asked, shining his flashlight down each path.

"I'm not sure," George said.

"Which way did they go?"

"I don't know."

They strained their ears against the night, listening over the buzzing katydids and chirping crickets. Then they heard the screaming again. This time it sounded like it was only a few yards up ahead.

"Come on!" George said, sprinting down the left trail. "This way!"

They followed the screams into the heart of the woods. With each new fork, the trail became sparser.

"Hold on, guys!" Peter yelled from behind. "Wait!"

The four friends stopped. "What is it?" George asked.

"I think they're behind us again."

"Behind us? But the trail goes this way," John said, pointing to the right.

"No, look," Abby said, "it goes straight."

"Are you sure?" Peter asked.

"Well, I thought I was."

"Wait a minute," John said. "The screaming stopped."

The four friends listened.

"You're right," George said. "I can't hear anything except the katydids."

"Where do you think they went?" Abby asked.

"I think we should go back," Peter said. "We're pretty far into the woods. I think we must have lost them."

"Or they lost us," George said.

"When I see those two butt-chompers again," Abby said. "I'm going to . . ."

The growl came from behind them. It turned from a low and raspy roar into a resonant howl. That's when something hit George in the face. It staggered him backward and made him drop his flashlight. It was leathery and wet and felt almost like a well-worn baseball glove. He picked up his flashlight and searched the ground for the object. The beam of light swirled in the weeds.

The growling circled them in the dark, edging closer and closer, and the four friends huddled together. Again, something leathery and wet flew out of the woods. This time it hit Abby from behind. She screamed.

"What was that!"

"I don't know! I don't know!"

The circle of light from George's flashlight came to rest on something that looked out of place in the underbrush. Was it the object that had hit him? His heart stopped. The object was half hidden beneath a fern. It was something small, something bloody. All he could think about was the Davison's goat, lying in pieces on the ground. He lifted the serrated leaf and looked at the hideous thing that had hit him. His eyes widened in horror. It was a hand. A small, white hand wet with blood. It looked as if it had been ripped off at the wrist. A pale jagged bone protruded from the bloody stump. That's when George started to scream.

19.

THE FOUR friends held each other in a fearful huddle, scream-ing at the bloody mess of a hand laying in a trembling circle of light. None of them could take their eyes off it: the paleness of its skin, the jaggedness of the bone, the crusted blood under its fingernails, and the abandoned ring on the ownerless ring finger.

Abby searched the ground for the gruesome thing that had struck her in the back. Part of her hoped she wouldn't find it, yet something inside compelled her to look. The white beam of her flashlight criss-crossed the emerald ferns and amber brown pine needles blanketing the forest floor. Then she saw it. It had come to rest on a rock a few feet away.

She didn't want to go near it, and still, she walked toward it. Her whole being shouted at her to stay away. It was as if she feared it would come to life and crawl toward her. She stepped forward, closer and closer, drawn by some primal urge, the horrible urge to *know*. She had to *know*. She had to find out what *it was*, even if it haunted her for the rest of her days.

She saw it now. She saw its size and its shape, and still, she didn't know. It was as if her mind had kept her from understanding, protect-ing her from the horrible fate of *knowing*. But it was too late. She screamed. It was another hand—most likely *the* other hand. Her eyes fixated on it: the paleness of its skin, the jaggedness of the bone, the crusted blood under its fingernails, and the abandoned ring . . .

"What?" She bent down to pick up the hand.

"Abby no! Don't!"

"It's fake!" she said, picking up the hand.

"What?"

She held it up so they could see. It flopped over in the middle like a dead fish. "Look. It's exactly the same as the other one!"

George bent down and picked up the hand that had hit him in the face. "It's rubber," he said, "and this blood smells like strawberry jelly!"

The rubber hands were the same, right down to the $1.99 price tag on the palm.

"Ah, nuts!" Peter said.

Seth and Jerry emerged from the woods, laughing.

"You booger toads!" Abby said.

John walked over and took the hand from Abby.

"We thought something was really wrong," George said. "Why would you do that to us?"

"If we couldn't scare you into leaving," Seth said, "we thought we'd at least teach you a lesson."

"Yeah," Jerry said, holding up an empty coffee can to his mouth. "Grrr, Owooo!"

"So that's why it sounded all echoey!" Peter said.

"I knew it!" Abby said.

"Are you guys crazy?" George asked. "You led us all the way out here in the woods for a joke?"

"Calm down, Georgie-poo."

John looked at the rubber hand. Then he bent down to inspect the ground where Abby found it resting on the rock.

"I knew you guys wouldn't play fair," George said, "but I didn't think you were stupid!"

"Uh, guys?" John said.

"Watch it, Georgie-poo, or you'll end up looking like that hand!" Seth said.

"Yeah, Georgie-poo," his sidekick agreed.

"Hey, guys!" John said, trying to get their attention. "I think you had better come look at this."

John knelt above the rock where Abby found the rubber hand.

"What is it, John?" George asked.

"This . . . uhm, rock."

"What about it?" Abby asked.

"I don't think it's a rock."

"Then what is it, Johnny boy?" Jerry said, mocking him.

"I think it's a bone."

"A bone?" Seth said, joining Jerry's taunts. "It's not a bone."

"No, not . . . not a bone, well, sort of," John said.

"What are you talking about, Johnny boy?"

"I think it's . . . a skull."

20.

THE BONE-WHITE dome of the skull lay half-hidden beneath a layer of amber brown pine needles. John pushed aside the needles to reveal the dark hollow sockets of some forlorn creature. He staggered backward through the bushes as the emptiness of its vacant stare gripped him.

"What is it?" Peter asked as the four friends crowded around the skull.

"It doesn't look human," Jerry said, pushing his way to the front.

"Yeah, it looks more like an alien," Seth said, joining his sidekick.

Seth grabbed a random stick from the ground and shoved it into one of the dark eye sockets. He lifted the skull from the matted layer of rotten foliage, revealing a large snout and two protruding fangs. Beneath the plant litter lay the decayed ribcage and front limbs of a small, tragic creature.

"I think it was a bobcat," George said, removing the disposable camera from his backpack.

"Ewe," Abby said, turning away.

Seth pushed away the rest of the rotting debris with the stick, exposing the interlocking bones of a twisted tail. George snapped a picture, illuminating the area in a blue flash.

"It's a bobcat all right," Seth said. "Look at the claws."

Abby glanced over her shoulder. "I think we should go," she said.

"Abby's right. I don't think we should stay here," George said, storing the camera and removing his flashlight again.

"Guys, I think you'd better look at this," John called from a few feet away.

The four friends pushed through the bushes and found John standing in the middle of a small clearing.

"Look," he said, shining his flashlight on the ground beside him.

The friends focused their beams on a small pile of bones. Some were broken into unrecognizable pieces. Others remained intact save for a few nicks and scratches.

"They look like they've been gnawed on," Peter said.

Seth and Jerry emerged through the shrubs. "What are you guys doing?" George pointed to the pile.

"Ah, it's nothing, you losers," Jerry said, "just another dead animal."

"John," George said, shining his flashlight at George's feet. "Look where you're standing!"

John lifted his sneaker. A layer of broken bones littered the ground.

"Oh," John said, "I thought they were pine needles."

The light from the four friends' flashlights revealed thousands of pieces of shattered and crushed bones.

"What is this place?" Peter asked, not really wanting the answer.

"I don't think a bear or a mountain lion would do this," Abby said.

The four friends panned the narrow beams from their flashlights around the clearing. Among the piles and shattered fragments lay several skeletons. Most were about the size of a raccoon or a fox; others, however, were much larger.

"There have to be dozens of them," Peter said.

"Look!" Abby yelled, shining her flashlight on a thicket of raspberry bushes. Several strands of coarse black hair hung from the thorny canes.

"It's just like we found in the woods outside the cabin!" Peter said.

"What are you guys talking about?" Seth asked.

"Not now, Seth," George said. He moved his flashlight back and forth over the pine needles. "There," he said, shining the beam of light on a bare patch of ground.

"Pawprints," John said.

"Just like we found outside the cabin," George replied.

"Bones, hair, paw prints," John said, adding things up for a deduction.

"We're in the creature's hunting ground," George said before John could finish.

John connected the dots in his head and nodded. His eyes looked fearful. "Yeah," he agreed, "right in the heart of its territory."

"We need to get out of here," Abby insisted.

George leveled his flashlight to illuminate the darkness beneath the branches of a dark thicket. "Oh no," he said. There, beneath the underbrush, lay the half-eaten remains of a large animal. Blood oozed from the long horrendous gashes on the animal's back, creating a ghastly red pool on the ground. "Uh, guys," George said, edging his way toward the animal for a better look, "these wounds are still fresh."

"Fresh?" Abby said.

"Yeah, I mean, it looks like this just happened." George caught his breath. "Whatever it was that killed that thing has to be close!"

The four friends stood with their backs together and turned their flashlights to the woods. The narrow beams of light pushed out against the darkness.

"What are you losers doing? There's nothing out there!" Seth said, sounding almost like he was trying to convince himself. "We've been running around out here for hours!"

That's when the crickets and katydids stopped.

21.

"OH, NO," George whispered.

"What?" Abby asked.

"It's too late."

"What do you mean?"

"It's coming."

"How do you know?"

"Listen."

"I don't hear anything," John replied.

"That's just it. The crickets and katydids have been buzzing and chirping all night, even when we were chasing Seth and Jerry. Now they've stopped."

The friends listened.

"He's right," Peter whispered. "I noticed it, too."

"What are you morons talking about?" Seth said.

"Shhh, Seth, keep your voice down."

"Don't tell me what to . . ."

The growl echoed in the darkness. At first, George thought it was Seth and Jerry trying to trick them again, but that was impossible. They were standing right in front of him. What's more, this wasn't a contrived metallic sound, like the howl that had come from Jerry's coffee can. Nor was it the heart-wrenching cry of some lost and desperate cat, like they had heard when Jeepers had wandered out of the woods the previous night. This was something else.

It was a deep and guttural sound that overwhelmed the emptiness of the night. It seeped from every pore in the earth and resonated from every rotting tree. It was an ancient and mournful sound, the sound of a creature that lived its wretched existence in darkness. It was the kind of sound you only hear once because it was the sound of approaching death.

The gravelly growl sputtered and grew, and the frightened friends flailed about with their flashlights trying to find the source. They twisted and turned in the dark, shining their beams this way and that, and still, they couldn't find the beast. Then, in a chaotic rush of a fierce and brutal force, the forest exploded in a clamor of splintering saplings and snapping limbs.

The friends leveled their flashlights in the direction of the commotion. The beams fused into a bright ray of light. It was then that they realized that they had made a horrible mistake. What were they thinking? Why had they come? What were they doing in the woods? Why did they have to know? But it was too late. They were there, and now they knew. If they lived through that moment, they would never be the same again. The sight of that hideous creature would stay with them and haunt their memories until the end of their days. It had started with something so innocent, a harmless curiosity, and a desire to know. But if they could go back they would ask themselves: *do you really want to know? Are you ready for the burden of knowing?*

The creature they had been searching for had revealed itself, and the four friends learned the horrifying truth. It wasn't a bear, or a mountain lion, or even a wolf. This was something wholly unknown to them, unknown to the world, a creature whose existence was not only unproven but unimaginable. Was it the Howler? Maybe, but they couldn't say for sure. The Howler was something they could understand. This was something much more terrifying.

22.

THE CREATURE skidded to a stop and turned from the light, its massive back heaving in heavy breaths. It reared and released a spine-tingling roar that turned the kids' blood to ice, and the four friends faced the full horrifying view of the beast.

It was undeniably huge, and although it ran on all fours using its powerful shoulders to plow through the trees, when it stopped it stood somewhat upright on its hind legs. Its back scraped the lower limbs of the canopy. It had a large round head like a grizzly, but its face and ears had the appearance of a wolf. Its body was covered with the same coarse black hair that the friends had seen clinging to the tree branches, but its snout was grotesquely bare. Gray drool seeped from its teeth and dripped from its monstrous muzzle.

The creature glared at the kids through dark inset eyes that reflected red in the beams of their flashlights. It shielded its face with a dark, bloody paw, which held the shape of a wolf's but with the protruding black claws of a bear. The claws bore the same pattern as the slashes they had seen on Jeepers and on the cabin door. The creature sucked the night air through its saliva-soaked teeth and filled its lungs like a bellows. Then it exhaled in a tremendous roar that flapped its heavy jowls. In an instant, the beast disappeared into the undergrowth, and the four friends searched for it frantically with their flashlights. It moved from shadow to shadow, circling out of range of their light beams.

"Where'd it go! Where'd it go!" John yelled.

"I don't know!" Peter replied.

George gripped his hatchet and prepared for the worst. He looked at Peter, who stood holding his empty slingshot, the rubber cord jumped and shook in his trembling hand. He would have to drop his flashlight to load a rock into the leather pouch. John picked frantically at the half-moon shaped groove along the metal edge of his pocketknife, but he couldn't get the blade to open. Abby moved her shoulders following the movements of the underbrush, her finger at the ready on the trigger of the pepper spray.

"Peter," Abby whispered, steadying her flashlight, "on the count of three I want you to load your slingshot."

"Uh, I . . . I . . . don't want to um, m-m-make it m-m-mad," Peter said.

"It's already mad. One . . . two . . ."

"Wait a minute," George said. "Don't move. I don't think it can see us."

"What do you mean?"

"Did you notice the way it turned from the light? I think it's almost blind. The light hurts its eyes." The beast edged closer through the brush and let out a blood-curdling howl. "Don't make a sound, and no one move," George said. He bent down and picked up a rock. Then he tossed it as far as he could into the woods. It landed with a thud, and the creature leaped toward it with a terrifying force. Seth and Jerry screamed.

"Arrgh!"

The two bullies took off through the woods, leaving the four younger kids behind. They knocked John's flashlight from his hands as they ran by. It landed with a crack then flashed to black in a blue spark.

"Seth! Jerry! No!" George screamed.

But it was too late. The creature turned and lunged after them.

Abby pressed the trigger, releasing a jet of pepper spray. It streamed haphazardly, distracting the beast. Peter dropped his flashlight to free his hand and grabbed a bone from the small pile. He loaded it into his slingshot, drew back on the band, and sent it sailing into the woods, away from Seth and Jerry. The creature turned, confused. But Seth and Jerry screamed again, and the creature ran after them in the darkness. George, John, Peter, and Abby ran the other way.

23.

THE FOUR friends careened through the woods with the under-brush slapping against their bare legs. The creature's bellowing howls and Seth and Jerry's desperate cries echoed in the night, sometimes close, other times farther away. It was as if the two bullies were running zigzags.

Deeper and deeper the friends fled into the woods, twisting and turning to avoid the horror that had befallen them. George looked over his shoulder at his three friends, Abby at his side, John and Peter at his heels. Seth and Jerry's screams and the howling had faded, and the crickets and katydids had returned. George stopped.

"Guys, hold up," he said, trying to catch his breath. "I think we lost it."

"Oh my gosh! Oh my gosh!" Peter said panting. "What are we going to do? That thing tried to kill us!"

"Keep your voice down."

"Right, sorry."

"I think we're safe."

"For now," Abby replied.

John rested his hands on his knees. "I knew it!" he said. "A cryptid. The Howler's a cryptid."

"Did you get a good look at it?" Peter said. "It was huge. It looked like a cross between a bear and a wolf."

"Bears and wolfs don't walk upright," John said.

"Bears do, sometimes."

"That thing's a monster," Abby said.

"Well, whatever it is," George replied, "we've got to get away from it."

"What about Seth and Jerry?" John asked.

The four friends looked into the dark woods.

George shook his head. "I don't know. I guess they're on their own." He slipped the backpack from his shoulders. "Quick! Give me some light."

"Mine's busted," John said, trying his flashlight. "Seth and Jerry knocked it out of my hands when they took off."

"Oh no," Peter said fumbling through the empty pocket where he kept his flashlight.

"What?"

"I dropped mine while I was loading the slingshot. I must have left it back there."

"Here," Abby said, shining the light from her flashlight on George's backpack.

George removed the map and the compass.

"Nuts," George said.

"What's wrong?"

He showed her the compass. "It's shattered. I must have banged it on a tree or something."

"Great."

"Now what'll we do?" John asked. "We're lost."

George looked at the survival patches on his backpack. "First, we don't panic. If we keep our heads, we may get out of this alive."

"That doesn't sound too promising."

"Second, we have to keep a positive attitude. We've made it this far."

"George is right," Abby said. "We can do this."

"Third, let's take a quick inventory. How many working flashlights do we have?"

"Two," Abby said, "yours and mine."

"Okay, and I've got extra batteries. Everyone check your backpacks to make sure they're zipped up, and everything's secure."

They inspected their packs.

"Check," Abby said.

"I'm good," Peter replied.

"Me, too," John said.

George paused. The woods were still and dark. The crickets and katydids hummed their night sounds. "If we're going to get out of here, we have to be smart. We need to use the forest to our advantage."

"What do you mean?" Abby asked.

"We need to be aware of our surroundings. We can't just go wandering into some predator's territory like we did last time."

"Yeah," John said, "that was stupid."

"The crickets and katydids seem to be able to tell when the Howler's around. They'll warn us."

"At least they'll know before we do," John said.

"Right."

"But how are we going to get out of here?" Peter asked.

George looked at the map. "I can get us back if I can pinpoint where we are."

SNAP! A dry limb cracked in the distance, and the crickets and katydids fell silent.

"What was that?" Peter asked as the night creatures resumed their persistent chirps and buzzes.

"It couldn't be the Howler. I still hear the katydids," George said.

The faint crunch of dry leaves murmured in the darkness.

"There it is again," John whispered.

"Someone's coming," Peter said.

"Or some*thing*," Abby replied.

"Peter load your slingshot."

Peter looked for a stone to fit the leather pouch. He found one about the size of a walnut.

Abby shook her pepper spray. "I think the can is empty," she said. She leveled her flashlight toward the sound. Bushes swayed in the undergrowth near the edge of the beam.

"What do we do?" Peter asked.

"We don't have a choice," George said. "We stand our ground."

24.

THE THING coming toward them approached faster now, moving through the brush at a steady pace. George removed the hatchet from its sheath, while Peter pulled back on his slingshot. John gripped his small pocketknife, and Abby held the flashlight. She fumbled it as she threw the empty can of pepper spray on the ground. The beam bounced off target.

"Wait a minute," George said, noticing the beam. "Abby turn off the flashlight."

"What? Are you crazy?"

"Just do it. Trust me."

Abby turned off the light, and the rustling in the underbrush ceased.

"Peter," George whispered, "shoot your rock."

Peter drew back the sling. He released a rock and sent it hurling into the night. It hit with a thud. *Umph!*

"Ow!" Someone cried from the undergrowth. "Why'd you do that?"

It was Seth and Jerry. Abby and George turned their flashlights on again.

"We thought you were the Howler," Peter said.

"Why are you butt-chompers sneaking up on us?" Abby asked.

"We weren't. It was dark," Seth said. His voice had lost its usual abrasive tone and taken on a toddler-like whine.

"We saw the light from your flashlight," Jerry replied.

"How'd you get away?"

"I . . . uh . . . I don't know," Seth replied. "Do you guys know how to get out of here?" His eyes shifted back and forth, scanning the woods. A cricket buzzed nearby, and Seth jumped. "What was that!"

"Seth, focus," Abby said. "Tell us. How did you escape?"

"We just kept running and changing directions until we lost it."

"Can we stay with you guys?" Jerry pleaded.

"You mean it just stopped chasing you?" Abby asked.

"I don't know . . . Yeah, I guess."

"That doesn't make sense," George replied.

"Unless," John added, "it wanted us to come this way."

"Why would it want us to do that?" Seth asked.

The four friends stood in silence, letting the question sink in. The dark woods pushed in all around them.

"What are we going to do?" Seth asked.

The four friends looked at him, puzzled.

George returned to the map. "We've got to figure out where we are," he said.

"George is right," Abby said. "We can't just go wandering around out here. We need to use our brains."

"We should spread out to see if we can find some landmarks," George said, "and we need to do it fast before that thing comes back."

"No way, I'm not wandering around out here alone," Jerry said, on the verge of tears. "What if we run into it again?"

"We'll go in pairs, and we won't go far. Just a dozen or so yards in each direction."

"It's going to be difficult with only two flashlights," John said.

"Two of us will stay here. This will be our base."

"No," Jerry said. "I won't do it!"

"Don't be such a baby, Jerry!" Abby said.

"Shut up."

"Guys, stop!" George said. "We can't start arguing amongst our-selves. Seth and Jerry, you guys stay here. Abby and I will go in one direction; John and Peter, you go in the other. Remember, only go a few yards—and listen to the crickets and katydids. If they stop, get your butts back here fast."

"What do you mean?" Seth asked.

"The Howler lives in the dark, so it uses its ears to find its prey. The crickets and katydids can tell when it's coming."

"Oh yeah, right," Seth said.

"Okay, guys, everyone ready?" They nodded. "Okay then, let's go."

25.

THE WHITE beam from George's flashlight pierced the darkness as he and Abby searched for clues that would lead them out of the woods and back to camp. A few steps behind them, Seth and Jerry sat with their backs pressed against the trunk of a large white oak. George swung the beam of his flashlight around to double-check their location. He could see the light from Peter and John's flashlight reflected against the low branches of the understory in the distance.

After a few yards, the thick underbrush thinned to a sparse stand of pine trees, allowing George and Abby to peer farther into the woods. George scanned the area with his flashlight. Large gray boulders protruded from the reddish-brown pine needles covering the ground. A sinking feeling came over George when he saw them.

"Oh, no," he said, stopping in his tracks.

"What is it?" Abby replied.

"See the terrain?"

"What do you mean?"

"The landscape. There aren't as many shrubs around here because we're deep into the woods where it's hard for the sunlight to reach the ground, and see those boulders over there?"

"Yeah?"

"That means we're close to the rocky cliffs of Calamity Hollow."

"Nuts," Abby said.

"Right."

George and Abby's world turned to black. The flashlight had flared and winked out. They gasped. No moonlight could reach them through the thick canopy of the pine trees, and the two kids stood vulnerable in the darkness.

"Uh oh," George said. He flicked the switch and tapped the side of the flashlight with his palm, but it wouldn't light.

"Give it to me," Abby said.

She fumbled for the flashlight and unscrewed the lens, being careful not to drop the pieces in the dark. She rearranged the batteries and inserted them back into the flashlight. To their relief, it turned back on, but it was strained and much dimmer now. Abby shined the flickering light around the grove of trees, to be sure they were still alone. They saw nothing but green pines and rocks.

"We'd better head back," George said, "see if John and Peter found anything. I'll put new batteries in the flashlight when we get there."

When they reached the white oak, John and Peter were waiting for them with Seth and Jerry.

"What'd you find?" George asked.

"There's a huge boulder near a break in the trees not far from here," Peter said.

"We may be able to get a better view if we climb it, but I think it's too tall," John added.

John and Peter led George to a boulder about the size of a box truck. John was right. It was much too tall for them to climb. George circled it, trying to get a glimpse of the nighttime sky through the opening in the treetops.

"Do you see it?" John asked.

"No."

"See what?" Peter asked.

"The Big Dipper."

"Why are you looking for that?"

"If we can find the Big Dipper, we'll be able to find the North Star. Then we just may be able to find our way out of here," John said.

"Oh, right," Peter said.

"Any luck?" Abby asked when they returned to the white oak.

"No," George said, removing the map from his backpack. "But I've got a pretty good idea where we are—and it's not good."

"So you can get us out of here then?" Seth asked.

"It's not that easy," George said, unfolding the map. "Look." They crowded around George so they could see. Abby angled the flashlight above the map. "This is Camp Calamity, right here," George said, pointing to the rectangular shapes outlining the cabins around Lake Mongoose. "You see this S-shaped ravine over here?" He pointed to something that looked like a dark, jagged scar. "That's Calamity Hollow. The gray boulders we've been finding mean we're pretty close. The Hollow is strictly off-limits in all the guidebooks—and that's not because the Howler lives there. It's because the terrain is extremely dangerous. There's only one way in and one way out, and it's surrounded by steep cliffs on three sides."

"Can't we just go back the way we came?" Jerry asked.

"But which way is that?" Peter replied.

"Let's say we're here," George said, pointing to the southern part of the map, near the bottom of the scar that marked the Hollow. "If we're here, then the way out is west. We can circle around the entrance to the Hollow."

"Well, that settles it," Seth said. "Which way is west?"

"No, Seth, that's not what I mean. Don't you get it? I said *if.* That's *if* we're near the entrance to the Hollow. If we're not, and we're north," George said, pointing to the opposite side of the Hollow, near the top of the S-curve, "then the way out is east."

"What are you saying, Georgie?"

"What I'm saying is, if we head in the wrong direction, we could be in deep trouble. We risk falling off a cliff and into the Hollow. I think we'll have a better chance of getting out of here if we wait until daylight."

"No way," Jerry said. "I'm not staying here! That thing is out there! It's coming back. I can feel it!"

"Me neither," Seth said, agreeing with his sidekick.

"Guys, listen," George said, trying to reason with them. "It's too dangerous. The cliffs on either side of the Hollow are extremely steep and drop off unexpectedly. They're even difficult to see in the daylight. One wrong turn and we're done for."

"We're done for anyway if that thing comes back," Seth said.

"Seth, Jerry, listen," Abby said. "George knows what he's talking about. He's got more experience than any of us out here."

"No, he doesn't! He's a loser!" Seth said. "I'm the only one who can get us out of here!"

"I agree with George and Abby," John said. "I think it's smarter if we stay. We know the Howler's afraid of the light—or that it at least hurts its eyes. We can find a good place to build a fire and take turns keeping watch."

"I agree," Peter said. "We can't just head off into the woods without knowing where we're going. If that thing traps us or chases us over a cliff, we're dead."

"We'll be dead anyway if it comes back!" Jerry said.

"Jerry and I are leaving!" Seth said. "Who's coming with us?"

The four friends looked at each other. They had no intention of splitting up or leaving with Seth and Jerry.

"Fine!" Seth said. "We'll go alone! We just need a flashlight!" He ripped the flashlight from George's hand.

"Seth that flashlight's—"

"Shut up, Georgie!" Seth said, cutting him off. "I'm taking it, and you can't stop me!"

"But Seth— "

Seth grabbed George by the shirt and twisted it tightly.

"Seth, don't!" Abby said. "Let him go." Seth pushed George to the ground. "Just let him take it, George," Abby said, helping him up. "He deserves everything he gets."

Seth smirked. "Come on, Jerry. Let's go."

The two bullies headed off into the woods.

"Guys, please," George said. "Stay with us."

"Forget it, George," John said.

It was no use. The bullies wouldn't listen. They disappeared into the overgrowth.

"Now what'll we do?" Peter asked.

"We're sticking to George's plan," Abby said.

"First, we need to find a good spot to spend the night," George said.

"Right. Then we need to make a fire—and fast," John added. "If that thing's trying to push us into the Hollow, it's sure to be back when it realizes we're not cooperating, and I don't know if the one flashlight we have left will be bright enough to fend it off."

"I think we should set up in the middle of the grove of pine trees," George said. "That way we'll see it coming."

26.

SETH AND Jerry found a narrow deer trail and followed it through the overgrowth, taking it deep into the woods. Soon, the underbrush thinned, and the trail disappeared. A wave of exhaustion settled over them. It weighed on their shoulders and made their arms feel like dumbbells. The arches in their feet ached, and their thighs burned. They stumbled and tripped over the hidden edges of gray boulders protruding from the ground.

Seth banged the flickering flashlight in his hand. The crickets and katydids hummed.

"This flashlight sucks!" Seth said. "That loser Georgie knew it didn't work. He *knew* it! That's why he let me take it. I'm going to kill him when I see him again."

"I can't see anything," Jerry said, stumbling again. "It's too dark, and there are too many rocks underneath these pine needles."

"Quit your whining, Jerry," Seth said. He smacked the blinking flashlight against his thigh. Then he turned the dim beam of light in each direction, but nothing looked familiar. The trees, rocks, and pine needles all looked the same. Everything had taken on the same vague randomness of the forest.

"I'm going to kill that Georgie when I see him," Seth said. "He knew this would happen. He *knew* it!"

"Which way do we go, Seth?"

Seth hesitated. "It's . . . it's this way," he said, motioning forward.

"Are you sure?"

"I . . . I don't know."

"We're lost. Aren't we, Seth?"

"Shut up! We're not lost. We're getting close. I just know it."

"I thought you said you could get us out of here."

"I said shut up and quit your complaining! I told you I would get us back to Camp Calamity and I'm going to do it!"

A low growl echoed somewhere in the distance. The crickets and katydids stopped.

"Did you hear that?" Seth whispered, turning around. The blood drained from his face, and his eyes widened.

"Oh no," Jerry said on the verge of tears. "That *thing* is coming, isn't it?"

Seth started to run. "Come on, let's get out of here!"

"Wait! Seth!" Jerry said in a panic. "Not that way! That's where the growling came from!"

"No," Seth said. "It came from the other way!"

"Seth, I think we should go back the way we came, see if we can find George and the others."

Seth paced, unsure of which way to go. "No way, I'm not going back," he said. "We're better off without those losers! We can get out of here by ourselves. I know it. We just have to keep going!"

A second growl echoed through the woods. It sputtered and groaned like the hinges of a graveyard gate.

An uncontrollable whine emerged from Jerry, and his eyes brimmed with tears. "It's getting closer, Seth," he said between whimpers. "We've gotta get out of here."

Something buzzed in front of them, making Seth turn. "Wait," he said. "Did you hear that?"

Jerry darted his teary eyes back and forth. "What?" he asked.

"Up ahead, the crickets and katydids. Remember what George said? As long as we can hear them, we'll be alright. Somehow they know when the Howler is close. If they're still buzzing in front of us, that means the Howler must be behind us."

"Are you sure?" Jerry asked, looking over his shoulder.

"I . . . I don't know," Seth replied. "I guess." He started in the direction of the crickets and katydids.

"Wait," Jerry pleaded. "Wha-wha-what if you're wrong? Wha-what if it wa-wa-wants us to go that way?"

"Don't be such a butt-chomper, Jerry. We just have to follow the buzzing until we find our way out. Now come on before that thing gets any closer."

Seth trudged through the woods.

"Okay," Jerry said, hurrying after him but still not convinced.

The two bullies followed the night sounds. Somewhere behind them, the creature lurked in the shadows. Calamity Hollow lay dead ahead.

27.

GEORGE, JOHN, Peter, and Abby stood on a carpet of pine needles in the middle of the grove of evergreens. It was the same grove that George and Abby had found earlier. The grove was filled with ancient trees with trunks the size of Greek columns. It would have taken all four of them, standing with their arms outstretched and their fingertips touching, to hug the circumference of the largest tree. No weeds or shrubs could grow there. Far aloft, the treetops unfolded in a thick canopy against the sky, blocking the sun by day and moon by night. Closer to the ground, the lower tree limbs hung just out of reach, which, when combined with the column-like tree trunks, gave the grove the appearance of a large room with a low-hanging ceiling.

"We need to find some twigs and branches to build a fire," George said. "These dry needles will do for tinder, but we need some larger sticks and logs to keep it going through the night."

"What about Seth and Jerry?" Peter asked.

"They won't make it very far with that flashlight," Abby said. "The batteries are almost dead."

George looked into the darkness in the direction the two bullies had gone. "We can't worry about them now," George replied. "They're on their own."

"Maybe they'll make it far enough that the light from the moon will light their way," John said without much hope.

George shook his head, still bothered that he couldn't convince them to stay. "Yeah," he said, "maybe."

"Come on," Abby said, tugging George by the arm, "we'd better get started."

The four friends worked in the narrow beam of the flashlight, gathering stray branches and sticks for the fire. It was the only working flashlight they had left, which made their progress slow. When their arms were full, and they struggled to keep a grip on their loads, they returned and made a pile near the center of the grove. They cleared the ground of pine needles. George kneeled and made a tepee of sticks. He found four logs about the size of baseball bats and set them aside. Then he made a pile of kindling, which he planned to use to feed the flames.

When he was satisfied with his preparations, George unzipped his backpack. He stopped when he saw the survival patches. He had been so irritated with his dad for making him earn them, and he had complained every minute while he was doing it. But now he realized that his father had been right, and he told himself that he would thank him when he got out of here—and *they would* get out of here.

George found his box of waterproof matches at the bottom of his backpack and stowed them away in the inside pocket for safekeeping. He made a mental note of where he put them. He would only use them as a last resort. Next, he found his flint fire starter kit, removed the magnesium rod from its pouch, and asked John to loan him his pocketknife. John unfolded the longest blade and handed it to George, who took it and scratched off a small pile of shavings about the size of a sugar packet. Then he struck the magnesium rod hard with the blade of the knife. The rod flashed in sparkler-like bursts of light and ignited the pile of shavings. The shavings set the tepee of sticks ablaze in a tongue of orange flame. George fed the flame with the kindling and watched as the fire smoldered and grew.

When he was sure the fire would burn without his prodding, George took the four baseball bat sized logs that he had set aside, trimmed off the bark with his hatchet, and notched one end of each of them in the shape of an X. He pried the notched ends open with a small stick and filled them with tinder. Then he stuffed them with as much wood shavings as he could and lit them. He handed the flaming torches to his friends, and they stood there in the flickering glow of the orange light.

"We need to make sure these never go out," George said. "We know that the Howler lives in the dark, so it uses its ears to find its prey. But we also know that it's afraid of the light—or at least that it hurts its eyes, so fire will be our first line of defense."

"If it gets close, aim for its eyes," Abby said.

"Right, good thinking—and stand still. Try not to make a sound."

"I'd rather not get too close," Peter said.

"Me neither," John agreed.

"We'll use the pine needles to make a ring of fire around the edge of the grove to keep it away," George said. "There's no brush here, so we should be able to see it coming from a good distance away."

"I'm not so sure about that," John said. "That thing has hidden in these woods for years—maybe even centuries. It might be able to sneak up on us. There's no telling what it can do."

"We need to stick together," Abby said. "Watch each other's backs."

"Right," George replied. "Good thinking. Abby, you and I will take one side of the grove and start making a fire ring around the perimeter. John, you and Peter take the other side."

"You got it, George."

"Listen for the crickets and katydids. If they stop their chirps and buzzes, get yourselves back to the bonfire right away."

George fed the bonfire until it illuminated the edges of the grove. Then the four friends fanned out around the perimeter, creating a circle of blazing light. When they finished, they returned to the bonfire to plan their next move. They set their torches in the fire to keep them lit.

"John, see if you can find a long, sturdy stick to use as a spear," George said.

"Right."

"Abby, go with him." He handed her his hatchet. "See if you can find a young sapling that's strong but flexible."

"Sure thing, George."

"What about me?" Peter asked as Abby and John headed off.

"Give me your backpack," George said.

Peter handed George the backpack. George emptied it and placed the contents in his. "Here," he said. "Fill this with as many round stones as you can carry. We need as much ammunition as we can get."

"Gotcha."

Abby and John returned with two short saplings that they had cropped off at the ground. Each one was about six feet long. George took the hatchet and trimmed off the leaves and sprouts. Then he cut off the end where the saplings started to taper. He removed the duct tape from his backpack and fastened John's open pocketknife to the end of the stick, wrapping the tape several times around to hold the open blade. He handed the newly-constructed spear to John.

"Here," he said, "take a few practice swings."

John took several hacks at the base of a tall pine.

"Try moving with a slashing motion," Abby said.

John took two swift swipes at the tree and inflicted several gaping wounds in the bark.

"Good," Abby said, "again!"

John slashed the tree again, leaving two more gashes. "I think I'm getting the hang of this," he said.

George took the other sapling and notched the ends with his hatchet. Then he thought for a moment.

"Peter? Do you still have your survival bracelet?"

"Yep," Peter said, holding out his wrist.

"Can I borrow it?"

"Sure, George," he said, unhooking the clasps, "that's why I brought it."

George unwove the cord and looped the ends. He tied it and hooked it over one of the ends of the sapling he just notched.

"Oh, I see what you're up to. That's ingenious, George," Abby said. "Give it to me. I'll finish it."

Abby took the branchless sapling and held it between her feet. Then she pulled it down to hook the other end of the loop and curved the sapling into a sturdy bow.

"Now all we need is arrows," Abby said, pulling on the string.

"I've got you covered."

George took about a dozen of the straightest sticks he could find, sharpened the ends, and notched the opposite sides to fit the string.

"What about the feathers?" Abby asked. "They won't fly straight without feathers."

George thought for a moment. "Hold on," he said. He removed the duct tape from his bag and ripped it into several short strips. Then he frayed the ends of the strips, to make them look like feathers, and slid them into the notched ends of the arrows.

"There," he said, "give it a try." Abby threaded a primitive arrow onto the bow and pulled back on the string. "Aim for the tree that Peter hacked, no use damaging another one." Abby let the arrow fly. It missed its target by only inches.

"The arrows aren't true," Abby said and pursed her lips. "But they'll work with a big target. Good work, George."

Peter returned with his backpack full of stones.

"Where's your slingshot?" George asked.

"Here," Peter said, handing him the slingshot.

"Put your backpack on backward so you can reach in the pocket from the front." Peter did. George handed him back the slingshot. "Now see if your arms can maneuver." Peter grabbed a smooth, round stone from the backpack and loaded it into the leather strap. "Can you move enough to fire?" George asked.

Peter pulled back on the sling and let the rock fly. "Yep," he said, "no problem."

Abby drew back on the bowstring and adjusted its tension. John swiped the air with his spear, and George hacked at an invisible target with his hatchet.

"Okay," George said. "I think we're ready."

The four friends took their positions, sitting with their backs to the flames on opposite sides of the fire. They waited. Somewhere in the darkness, the Howler closed in on its prey.

28.

SETH AND Jerry followed the sounds of chirping crickets and buzzing katydids through a thick grove of hemlock trees, which they viewed through an ever-weakening circle of white light. A short distance away, the creature pursued them. It lurked in the shadows, waiting for its chance to strike.

The flashlight Seth carried flickered and strained, struggling to suck the remaining volts of electric current from the batteries. In a final flare, the flashlight bulb winked out, and the two bullies stood in the unprotected shadow of night.

"Oh no," Jerry said as he started to cry again.

Seth slapped the flashlight in his palm in frustration, trying to coax one last ounce of juice from the batteries, but it was no use. They were dead.

"Now what'll we do?" Jerry asked in a whimper.

"I'm going to kill that Georgie," Seth said, blinking his eyes to try to adjust to the dark. A faint light from the moon filtered through the treetops. "Let's just keep going," he said. "I think we're almost out of the woods."

The two bullies plodded onward, straining their eyes to try to make sense of the purple shapes in front of them. They feared the shapes would turn into something sinister, something that would send them running for their lives. They moved from tree to tree, groping for them in the dark. They didn't know why the trees made them feel safe. They offered no refuge or place to hide. If the Howler should come and send them fleeing, there would be no real hope of escape.

Seth grabbed the next tree and steadied himself against the dark. He stared into the night, hoping to see something that would lead them back to camp. He watched as the dark forms in front of him hardened into familiar shapes—a tree, a shrub, a boulder, but he saw nothing that would lead them back to the upper field. He listened for the sounds of the crickets and katydids.

"Come on," he said when he heard them. But before he could reach the next tree, the crickets and katydids stopped, and the two bullies stood in cold silence.

The growl came from behind them. It was so close they could hear the saliva gurgling in the creature's throat.

Seth stopped, and Jerry slammed into his back.

"Umph!"

The creature released a scream from the pit of its stomach, leaving little doubt that it was the Howler. The sound shook the bullies' bones and rattled their teeth.

The bullies turned to see the horrid creature silhouetted against the moonlight. It was standing upright but hunched over, supporting the weight of its massive back. Its oversized claws dangled in front of it like a set of sharpened knives, and saliva dripped from its long snout.

"Come on!" Seth said, lunging to his right.

The two bullies ran through the woods as the creature pursued them in a fury. Trees and branches cracked and snapped behind them. The creature moved like an avalanche, consuming the forest in a fit of destruction. The bullies darted to the left and the right, dodging trees and the huge gray boulders that had become more prevalent now.

The Howler gained ground, but the bullies were too scared to look. They could feel its heavy footfalls rumbling the earth and the air moving through its bellows-like lungs. It smelled of death and decay. It was as if the creature had crawled from the hole in the world where the dead go.

Ahead of them, the woods brightened, and for a moment, the bullies thought they would escape. The trees around them thinned into a sparse grove, and moonlight appeared in the sky above a clearing.

"This way!" Seth yelled.

The two bullies picked up speed. With each step, the woods became brighter and brighter. They could see the clearing up ahead.

When they reached the tree line, the Howler lifted its monstrous paw and swatted.

"Argh!"

"Look out!"

The claw ripped through the back of Jerry's shirt. It hung in ribbons from his husky frame.

The bullies hurtled out of the woods. But instead of running into the upper field, they found themselves falling. They plummeted down a cliff, tumbling end over end. On and on they fell. Their limbs twisted and their bodies slammed against the earth. They slid to a stop at the bottom of a dark gorge. They lay there in a heap cradling their battered bones and moaning with mouthfuls of dirt. Above them, the moon darkened as clouds rolled across the sky.

The Howler stood at the edge of the precipice, peering down at its defenseless prey. Thunder rumbled in the distance. A drizzle had begun to fall, and the creature turned and slunk back into the woods. The night was young. The hunt had only begun, and several more victims waited in the woods.

29.

GEORGE, JOHN, Peter, and Abby sat with their backs to the bonfire and their weapons at the ready. They peered into the darkness, straining their eyes to look past the flaming ring of pine needles they had created around the outer edge of the grove. They searched for signs of movement and listened for an unknown sound. A shifting shadow or snapping twig could mean that the Howler had returned, and while the friends thought that they were ready, they didn't want to be surprised by the beast.

A cold rain fell, signaling the arrival of a summer storm. The rain rolled down the four friends' necks and sent shivers down their spines.

"Oh no," John said.

Thunder rumbled in the distance, releasing another kind of a chill.

"What was that?" Peter asked.

"Thunder," George replied.

"That's not good," Abby said.

"No, it's not. If these fires go out, we're in deep trouble."

"What'll we do?" Peter asked.

Lightning flashed, illuminating the woods in blue light. The thunder rumbled closer now.

"Come on!" George said, springing to his feet. "We've got to stoke the fire with all the wood we can!"

The four friends ran to the pile and threw all the sticks and logs they had collected onto the flames. The fire cracked and smoked with the new wood.

"Do you think it's enough?" Abby asked, throwing the remaining branches into the fire.

George shook his head. "It'll have to be. We may be alright beneath these pines."

"It might be okay in a drizzle," John said, sizing up the flames, "but I don't think it will last if it starts to pour."

The four friends picked up their weapons and waited. Within moments the empty quiet of the woods was filled with the growing white noise of coming rain. It muffled the songs of the crickets and katydids, and soon the sounds disappeared in the commotion of a cloudburst.

"Now what?" Abby yelled, straining to be heard above the din.

"Be ready," George said, clutching his hatchet. "Stay on your guard!"

The outside ring of fire hissed and fizzed in the rain. Part of the circle winked out in a patch of white smoke.

"John, Peter! Grab a torch and see what you can do over there!" George said.

John and Peter grabbed their torches and tried to relight the smoldering ring. They kicked dry needles on the areas that had been doused, trying to light them again. The needles flickered and smoldered in a sick flame.

While John and Peter fought with the outer ring, the bonfire in the center of the grove weakened. George and Abby poked and prodded at it with their torches. But it was no use. The clouds had released their loads, and a deluge of rain had begun to cascade through the cracks in the canopy.

Lightning flashed. John and Peter returned to help George and Abby with the bonfire. They noticed the other side of the fire ring had gone out, leaving them exposed to the darkness on one side.

"Look!" John yelled. "The fire ring! It's out!"

"It's no use!" Peter yelled as the bonfire in the center of the grove dimmed. "It's just too—"

The Howler exploded over the smoldering ring from the outer darkness, knocking John and Abby off their feet. It moved in a dark blur blending in with the shadows. Peter loaded a rock into his sling-shot and fired. It missed wildly and cracked into a tree. The creature's ears twitched, and it lunged toward the sound.

Abby pulled herself to her feet and grabbed the flashlight. "George, catch!" She threw the flashlight to George, who caught it with his free hand.

The Howler turned and raced toward Abby in a fitful rage. She screamed. George fumbled with the flashlight. He flicked it on in a panic and aimed it in the creature's eyes. Blinded, the creature missed, allowing Abby to scramble out of the way. It skidded to a stop, pawing at its face. Then it released a guttural roar that turned their blood cold.

John struggled to his feet and grabbed the makeshift spear. The tip jumped and shook in his trembling hands. The Howler's ears twitched again. It turned and charged at John, who slashed at the creature. John was sure he had wounded the beast, but the gash hadn't even pen-etrated the creature's hide. The pocketknife hung loosely at the end of the spear. John grabbed it and ripped it from the duct tape.

The Howler whirled around and bore down on John again. When it turned, George rushed in, screaming and swinging his hatchet. He landed a heavy blow on the creature's back. The creature howled in pain and swatted George with the back of its paw. He stumbled into a bush and scrambled to keep the beam fixed on the beast. The wounded Howler retreated to the shadows. It circled them out of range of the light.

John helped George to his feet, and the four friends stood shoulder to shoulder with their weapons ready.

"What'll we do?" Peter asked, loading another stone into the sling.

"We need more light!" Abby yelled as the last of the orange flames from the bonfire flickered out.

The creature lunged at the kids again, scattering them in differ-ent directions. John and Peter stood exposed in the dark. The creature charged them and swung its massive claw. John slashed at it helplessly with his pocketknife while Peter fired the stone from the slingshot.

Fearing for her two friends, Abby loaded an arrow into her bow and pulled back on the string. She released it, but it wobbled awkwardly off target.

"No!" Abby yelled as the arrow sailed into the darkness.

Lightning pierced the sky again, releasing a loud clap of thunder. The creature cowered and roared at the sky. George's eyes widened. He bent down and began shuffling through his backpack.

"George, what are you doing!"

"Just hold on!" He rummaged through his pack in a frenzy.

Peter loaded a rock into his slingshot and fired it at the creature. It landed hard below the Howler's temple. The creature roared as Peter tried to reload.

Then George found what he was seeking. He darted between the creature and his friends holding the disposable camera high above his head. He pressed down on the shutter, and the camera flashed with a blinding blue light. The Howler reared and roared, covering its eyes in pain. George ignited the flash again and again until finally he ran out of film and the camera ceased.

"Come on!" Abby yelled. She grabbed George by the arm, and the four friends ran from the grove.

The friends disappeared into the undergrowth and sprinted past the large white oak where they had last seen Seth and Jerry. They pushed through thickets of thorny limbs. The switches slapped their arms and sliced their bare legs. As they twisted and turned through the thicket, the creature bellowed in pain behind them. After several yards, the thicket thinned, and the shrubs gave way to large gray rocks and boulders. George shined the flashlight in each direction.

"Which way?" Peter asked.

George pressed his finger to his lips, silently pleading with Peter to stay quiet. Angered by its sudden blindness, the creature barreled after them, shredding through the forest like a storm.

As the rain fell harder upon their necks, pelting them with huge drops, George looked to the left and then the right. He was sure the clearing was near. The canopy had opened above them allowing more rain to pour through. Then he found what he was looking for: the large boulder the size of a box truck that John and Peter had found earlier. He grabbed his friends, and they hurtled toward the rock. Driven by a growing panic, the four friends ran faster and faster. But still, the creature gained ground, closing in behind them with breakneck speed.

When they reached the boulder, George froze. He kneeled and clasped his hands together. At first, his friends thought that he had given up and that he had stopped to say a final prayer. Then he opened his hands and motioned for Abby to proceed. She placed her foot in his hands, and George hoisted her to the top of the rock with all his might. He did the same with John and Peter.

The Howler was almost on them. On top of the rock, Abby loaded an arrow onto her bow, and Peter and John leaned over the edge, trying to save their friend. George jumped and stretched with all his might. But he couldn't reach them.

"Come on, George!"

"Jump!"

"I'm trying!"

Abby drew back on the bowstring, cradling it to the right of her nose. She would only have one chance to stop the creature, and she had to make her shot count. John and Peter scrambled beneath her feet, trying desperately to save George, who grasped for his two friends with his hands outstretched.

Abby tried to remain calm, but her heart felt like it was beating in her throat. The creature careened through the woods, exploding through the undergrowth in a fury. Abby focused her breath and aimed, but below her, George had started to panic. He jumped and clawed, trying to reach his friends. It was no use. He couldn't do it. The boulder was just too tall and his friends just out of reach.

The creature closed in on him, and George took two steps back.

"What are you doing!"

"George, come on!"

George ran toward his friends and jumped as hard as he could. Without warning, Peter lunged over the side. John grabbed his legs as he toppled over the edge. Peter grabbed George by the arm, and the two friends pulled George to safety. The three of them lay in a heap on top of the rock.

Abby aimed at the hideous Howler. She inhaled through her nose and exhaled through her mouth. Then she let the bowstring roll from her fingertips, and the arrow sailed through the air toward the charging beast.

30.

ABBY HAD remembered how the first arrow she had fired had missed and wobbled off target, so this time she compensated by aiming a few degrees to the right. She also aimed high, anticipating that the creature would lunge toward its prey. She was calm and sure. She thought of nothing but the tension of the bowstring and the path of her arrow.

Abby released the arrow as the Howler launched itself into the air. The arrow quivered as it flew toward its mark. When the Howler reached the apex of its jump, the arrow hit home and embedded itself in the creature's eye. The Howler slammed into the boulder and fell to the ground writhing in pain. Abby threaded another arrow onto her bowstring and fired. She struck the creature below the shoulder. It released an anguished howl and struggled to its feet. As Abby reached for another arrow to finish it, the Howler hurtled through the woods and disappeared into the night.

"Woohoo!"

"Yeah!"

"You did it!"

Abby grinned. "Thanks to George's quick thinking."

"What about me?" Peter asked. "I'm the one who saved him."

"Yeah, and I saved *you*," John replied.

"No, you didn't!"

"What do you think I was doing, picking boogers? You almost went over the edge!"

"I wouldn't have fallen."

"Guys quit it," George said.

"Yeah," Abby said. "How do we know it won't come back?"

"We don't," George replied. "But I think it's safe to say it won't be any time soon."

"I don't think we should be here if it does come back," Abby said. "I've only got one arrow left."

"I agree with Abby," Peter said. "I'm pretty much out of rocks."

"I've still got my pocketknife," John replied. "But I'd rather not get too close to that thing—especially since it's wounded."

George picked up the flashlight and shined it into the woods in the direction the Howler had fled. A goopy trail of blood marked its path.

"If the Howler's like other animals, it's probably heading back to its den in the Hollow," George said. He looked at the sky through the opening in the canopy. The rain had slowed to a drizzle, and the clouds raced overhead. "The clouds usually move in the direction of the prevailing winds from the west," George said. "That's the same direction the Howler went." He removed the map from his backpack. "If Calamity Hollow is west, that means the way back to camp is east, the same direction as the clouds and the opposite direction of the Howler."

"That sounds good to me," Abby said.

"Me, too," John and Peter said together.

"Jinx!"

"Cut it out, you two! We're not out of the woods yet."

"Haha, very funny."

"Abby's right," George said. "We still have to be on guard."

The four friends climbed down from the boulder and headed off in the direction of the moving clouds. They left the Howler and the trail of blood behind them.

31.

AGAIN, SETH tried to climb the rocky, steep-sided gorge that formed the eastern edge of the Hollow—this time taking a running start—and again he slid into the dark, muddy filth of the pit-like chasm where the Howler lived.

"No! No! No!" Seth screamed as he slid backward on his stomach through the muck. A brown scum flew as he slammed his fists to the ground in frustration.

Jerry sat in the same spot where the two bullies had come to rest earlier, inspecting the pieces of his frayed shirt. "Seth?" he whimpered as murky, tear-like trails dripped down his cheeks. "H-H-How are we gonna get out of here? Wha-wha-what if that *thing* comes back? What if it finds a way to get down here to get us!"

Seth grabbed a fistful of sludge and flung it at the canyon wall. Then he sat there with the corners of his mouth turned in a frown. He looked like a toddler who had missed his nap.

"Seth?

"Ah, shut up, Jerry!" Seth said as he started bawling. "Why don't you try something!" He grabbed another fistful of filth, but this time he just flung it in the air. It landed in clumps on the bullies' heads. He got up and started yelling.

"Help! Somebody help us! Please! Somebody! Help us!" He threw himself down in the sludge and sobbed again. When he wiped the tears from his cheek, he left a muddy smudge.

Lightning streaked across the sky in a clap of thunder, and the bullies jumped.

"Let's just go!" Jerry said, rising to his feet. "We can't just sit here! We need to get out of this storm—and we need to find a place to hide before *that thing* comes back!" It came out as more of a whine than a plan, so Seth just sat there crying.

As Jerry walked away, the drizzle turned into a downpour.

"Jerry wait!" Seth said, slipping on the sludge again. He got up and stumbled after Jerry. "Don't leave me here alone!"

The two bullies trudged through the mud, searching for a place to hide. Somewhere in the Hollow, the Howler hobbled back to its lair.

32.

WHILE JOHN and Peter searched the woods behind them, George put away his hatchet and boosted Abby up the trunk of a large oak.

"There it is," Peter said, shining the flashlight on a distant tree, which was wrapped in a ring of duct tape.

"Right on target," John replied.

Abby wrapped the duct tape around the oak and ripped it from the roll with her teeth. "Got it!"

George lowered Abby to the ground and took out the map. "It shouldn't be too much farther now," he said. "John, Peter, find another tree to mark our heading."

"Right."

Peter extended his arm and used his thumb to line up the two trees. He drew an imaginary arrow in the air between them to find a third tree on the same heading.

"There," John said, shining the flashlight about fifty yards in front of them. "That one. The Hemlock."

"Good work, guys," George said.

"Do you think we're going in the right direction?" Abby asked.

"We may be off by a couple of degrees, but I'm fairly confident we're still heading east."

Without a compass, landmarks, or stars to guide them, the hike back to Camp Calamity had been slow and tedious. But after they fell into a rhythm, the trek progressed much faster, until finally, they saw the familiar silhouettes of the lean-tos in the upper field.

The four friends sprinted from the woods.

"Look!" Peter said, jumping onto the platform of the last lean-to. "Seth and Jerry's backpacks! They're still here!"

"Uh oh, that's not good," John said.

"I guess they never made it back," Abby replied.

"What should we do? Should we go back out and look for them?"

"We can't go out there on our own—not in this weather, not while it's still dark."

"Come on!" George yelled as he darted across the field. "We've got to wake Counselor Jack!"

The four friends raced down the trail toward the cabins, splashing through mud puddles and dodging wet branches as they ran. The camp was eerily quiet. George thought it must be getting close to dawn, because the night sounds in the woods had ceased, even the loons along the lake were silent.

The friends took the stairs of Cabin 19 two-by-two and jerked open the tattered screen door. George stopped short when he entered the room, and his three friends slammed into his back. *Umph!*

The growl filled the cabin with a ghastly drone, and George reached for the hatchet on his belt. His stomach sank when he remembered he had repacked the hatchet in his backpack. It had gotten in the way when he was helping Abby mark the trees. It all came rushing back to him now: the shadow by the window, the footprints outside, the claw marks on the screen door . . .

"George! What are you doing?" Abby asked, scolding him.

The snarling continued in heavy breaths. Abby heard them at the same time she recognized the fear on George's face.

"George," she said, "it's okay. It's just Jack. He's snoring!"

"Oh," George said, sounding a little embarrassed.

The four friends rushed into the counselor's room. John grabbed Jack and shook him by the shirt.

"Jack, wake up."

Jack snorted and rolled over. John nudged him again. "Jack?"

"A few more minutes, mom," Jack said, slurring the words together.

"We don't have time for this," Abby said, pushing her way in front of John. She leaned in close to Jack's ear. "Hey, Jack!"

Jack shot up. "Huh? What?" He rubbed the back of his head in confusion. "What are you guys doing up?" he said. "It's still dark out." He sank back down beneath the covers.

"Jack, you don't understand. You've gotta help us," George said. "It's Seth and Jerry. They're lost in the woods."

"Who's lost?" Jack said in a mumble.

"Seth and Jerry. We were chased by the Howler, and now we can't find them."

"The Howler? Seth and Jerry?" Jack said, sounding more alert.

"Yeah, they're lost in the woods somewhere."

Jack rolled over and drew up the covers around his shoulders. "Ah, come on, guys. Go back to bed. They're probably just trying to scare you. They've already lost their privileges once for scaring kids down at the Kitty Cabins."

"Jack, no. It's true." Peter said. "You've got to believe us." But Jack was already snoring again. "Now what?"

The four friends looked at each other.

"How can we convince him that we're not joking?" Abby asked.

John put a hand on his chin. It was like the boy who cried wolf.

"George, what about your camera?" he said. "You must have gotten at least a dozen pictures when you zapped the Howler in the face."

"What am I supposed to do," he said, "find an all-night photo booth? I can't develop the film myself."

"Oh, yeah. Right."

"Wait a minute!" Peter said. "What about the game camera? It's digital. It has a screen on the back and everything!"

"It's worth a shot," Abby said.

"Come on!"

The four friends bolted out the door and raced toward the upper field. Thinking that the game camera had captured the Howler on film was a long shot, but they knew it was the only chance they had to save Seth and Jerry.

33.

SETH AND Jerry stumbled into the dark recesses of Calamity Hollow. A cold rain fell. It dripped down their backs, releasing shivers along their spine. The hair on their necks stood on end, and a harsh reality settled in: they were lost—and more than that, they were trapped. It was as if the Howler had planned it that way all along. It had separated them from their friends, driven them into the maze of the Hollow, and trapped them like feeder mice in a terrarium. It was only a matter of time before it returned for its fill.

A dark shadow appeared in the cleft of the rock wall. It was a cave, and Seth and Jerry's spirits lifted in a glimmer of hope. Perhaps they could escape the fate that awaited them—or at least hide until the coming of day. The bullies set their faces toward the cleft. They ducked their heads beneath the bluff and entered.

34.

ON THE western edge of the upper field, the four friends hurried down the path that led to the game camera. Peter found the tree and ripped the Velcro apart to loosen the straps.

"Come on, Peter. Hurry!" John said.

"Okay! I'm trying!"

Peter removed the camera and knelt on one knee. His friends pressed in around him, desperate to get a glimpse. He toggled the switches, and the screen lit up. A grayish light reflected off their faces.

"What's on it?" Abby asked. "Did it catch anything?"

"Hold on," Peter replied.

Peter pressed another button, and an image of the four friends running through the woods filled the screen.

"There!" Abby said. "That's us!"

"That's when we were chasing after Seth and Jerry!" John said.

Peter scrolled through the images one at a time. They saw pictures of a squirrel, a rabbit, and a bat.

"Is that it? Is that all there is?" John asked. The pictures seemed to be of little use.

Peter advanced through the images, speeding from one picture to the next, hurrying to get to the end.

"Wait, wait, wait!" George said as Peter raced through the images. "What was that? Go back!"

Peter stopped and reversed through the images. He flipped through them one by one. A cool light flashed on their faces.

"No, not that one," Peter said. "Keep going. There!"

Peter stopped.

Abby gasped and covered her mouth.

"Oh, my g . . ." Peter said.

"It's . . . a cryptid!" John replied. "I think we're going to be famous!"

George tugged on Peter's arm. "Come on!" he said. "We've got to get this to the counselors and fast!"

35.

A WARM breeze blew from the mouth of the cave, flowing from somewhere deep inside the earth.

"Seth, hurry!" Jerry said. "Before that thing comes back."

Seth strained his eyes against the darkness. "I can't see anything in here."

"Move to the back," Jerry pleaded. "I don't want that thing to find us." Seth shuffled his feet, edging deeper into the cave. He groped in the darkness, searching for the back wall.

"Why does it smell so bad in here?" Jerry whined.

Sweat dripped from Seth's forehead—or was it coming from somewhere on the ceiling? It felt slimy as it oozed down his cheek. He turned and nudged against the back wall. Why did it feel so hairy?

"Don't worry, Jerry," Seth said in a whimper. "If we're really quiet, it won't find us." That's when he felt the hot breath on the back of his neck, and the claws close in around his face.

ABOUT THE AUTHOR

JOE HARVEY is an English teacher, musician, and author of books for upper-grade children, teens, and young adults. He lives in Bethlehem, Pennsylvania with his wife, Kara, his children, Zachary and Erica, his Golden Retriever, Lola, and his two cats, Cinnamon and Sugar.

Made in the USA
Monee, IL
11 July 2020

35612178R00080